The Deep Green Sea

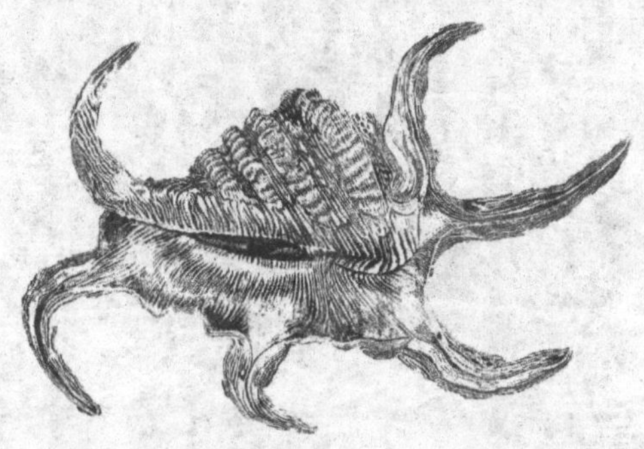

A Selkie Tale and Sacred Spiritual Journey

Written And Illustrated By

DR. KELSEY ASHE

DARK SWAN IMPRINT
Fremantle   Western Australia

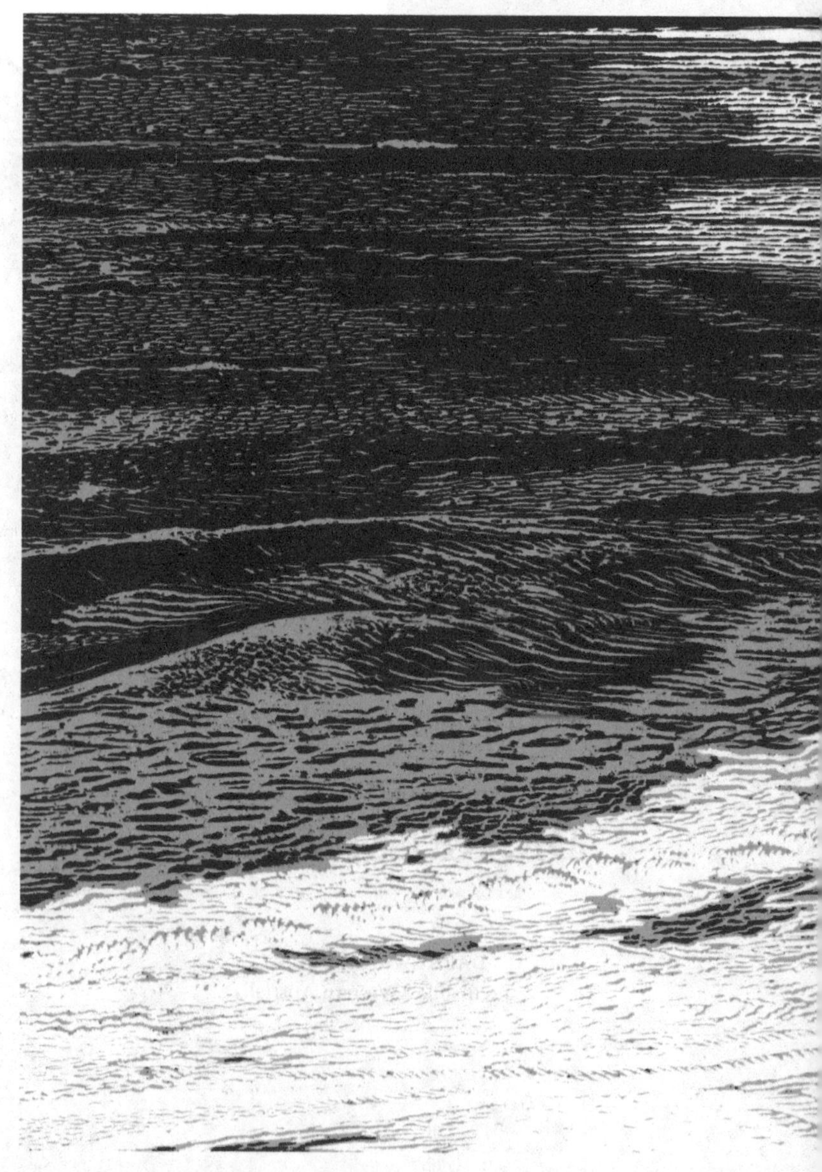

For my
daughter Delphi,
whose fierce soul
carried us both through
the deep green sea.

-

And for all who
have drifted into the
dark and found
their way home
again.

CONTENTS

VOCABULUM

ACOLYTE: *Those-in-Learning.* Refers to newly arrived seekers, inducted into the Mirage Isle Sanctuary. Assistants to the Adepts and High Priestesses' of the Isle.

ADEPT: *Those-Whom-Hold.* An individual who has attained a level of knowledge, skill, or aptitude in doctrines relevant to the Mirage. According to tradition, Adepts are marked by their ability to 'hold the thread' of the Sacred as they ascend toward Anchorite status.

ANCHORITE: *Those-Whom-Never-Leave.* Those who seek and attain permanent withdrawal from the world to live a life of seclusion and devotion to preserving the Sanctuary across Epochs.

ADORATRICE: *Keeper-of-the-Keys.* The Highest ranking of the seven High

Priestesses of the Mirage Isle, often holding the most significant power, influence and knowledge.

THE MIRAGE: A devotionary order of women who exist beyond the veil of customary sight. Guardians of ancient wisdom, protectors of the soul's evolutionary flame.

THE SECOND DELUGE: A cataclysmic event beginning circa 3400 A.D. (I), when the seas rose and reshaped the known world of Old Earth across millennia. This epoch witnessed Earth's brief resurgence, gradual decline, and eventual demise, and the founding of the Mirage Sanctuary around 4700 A.D. (II).

THE ARK CORACLE: A vessel built in preparation of sailing at the time of the Third Deluge, carrying forward the seeds of consciousness to establish New Earth.

The Last Acolyte
Orla. ENTRY №:01

Midwinter. 5277 A.D.II (After 2nd Deluge)

The voyage was nearing arrival. 12,000 nautical miles of cloud covered silence sunk into grey periphery. Facing down river towards the open sea, with wild-wind in wild-hair, I pressed my limbs firmly into the kernel of the barge's prow, allowing the weathered beams to cradle me like an anonymous friend. Leaning forward into the embrace, the masked veneer of ego's cold cheeks cracked and a deep exhale of surrender prised out from within.

Arteries and veins crept vine-like over a heart of stone, desperate for a place to grow. Pinching and clawing, then tangling into a mass of stinging punctures. A keening-song kept swooning up low in the chest, blending into the vibration of the boat engine. An in-tune rumbling hum of sorrow, involuntary and driven by catharsis.

The sound droned automatically from the mouth, instinctual and unstopping it continued, blending higher and louder. A monk-like reverb of hollow tone surged through the ship, through my whole frame, until all became one and I could hide under that sound.

Under crushing eyes, I saw then an image floating. A spinal column, intertwined like a tri-plaited rope of body, mind and spirit, with fibres frayed and tufted apart at top and bottom, yet still crimped with the recent grooves of its woven whole.

The vision came with new unchosen
sounds; not a voice, but a hard guttural
howl, so violent I could feel corrosive shards
upon my throat. I sent the growl low into
the grave of gut, forcing the burn to spell a
quiet masochism; *take control of this destruction
of beauty.*

Intimacies no longer contained, my cry
entwined up into the high-motor-hum,
lifting in liberation to the sea behind me,
flying off my shoulder into sprays of white.

Aaaaarrrrrrrrrrggggggggggghhhhhhhhhhhhh!

Letting go, I wailed high… A full-throttle
scream. A strange shrill echo scattering in
the crosswind. I imagined the giant old river
trees witnessing me at the prow like a
wounded figurehead, whistling through the
air.   I opened my arms as if to slice
through and raised my chin in defiance.

The initiation is underway.

Particles became present, whole structures formed and caved in my vision, time and the expanse of it flashed, 5 days, 5 years, 20 years, 100 years, 1000 years, 10,000 years, 100,000 years. Nothing, nothing, nothing, nothing.

Everything.

In rapid waves now. A caustic forming and unforming of words erupted in my mind…then another and another grinding pain gouged deep into the plexus. A searing-sickening acid-brick weighed there like a hotbed magnet, dragging in the pit of my body.

From the mouth-of-self, I purged grey liquid, with flecks of silver and copper. I purged charcoal, ink, cotton, paper. Up came the unconscious materials of my psychic depths. All vim expired, I broke, caving forward into the smooth limbs of the bow; a shuddering weep of flesh. Tears streamed horizontal across my face in blusters and a sea eagle circled, as if thirsty for them.

Behind me, on the boat for hours, the barge had been steady, noisy, pushing against the rushing-in-tide of the rivers' teeth, observing this dissolution. Moments of serenity and calm would return at times, euphoric, for

flashes....

Whole alcoves of blossoming flowers draped into the river's edge in shades of skin and wine in shocking beauty. Damp ferns huddled in clumps. The air became noticeably cleaner and calmer, the freshest I'd ever smelt; brackishly sweet and uplifting. It carried a stirring summons, something unnameable, rich and invisible...

An invitation.

I began to notice the clouds racing, pulled apart by light and haze. Something bright was beyond, I reached for it...this wholesome, complete, unified thing….It was hope, out on the horizon, calling me. I saw myself, as if from outside the body. The eyes twinkled, glassy.

Step aside, lean in…reach.

The perfection of the lowering sun over the river was undeniable, the position at the centre prow enviable. The light, the softness… the splintering of beauty.   My heart, black, blue, green, bruised. The trees, black, blue, green, purple. The wonder blistered me then, and I felt the pure joy of life.

What relief to perceive this sudden pleasure. The bird in the hand. The angel intervening. Consequences of loopholes in timelines. A slide sideways, in-between nowhere.

A semblance of the physical world returned. Eucalypt and salt coated tongue and hair. The white bellied sea eagle circled again, its eyes black stones falling on me.

I thought back on earlier, milder, moments of awakening. When the abyss stared back and the witness entered, with a message, then left and a clearer voice was discerned. I thought about the sequence of events that brought me to this moment, when logic fell away and this more subtle reality was revealed. I was now on the opposite pole of the Earth and if not for gravity, surely I'd float away.

"Are you okay love? Orla? Are you sea-sick Miss?"

A kind, voice behind me. The Boatswain, doing his job, caring for his cargo.

"I'm fine, really… I'm okay, thank you."

Denial equals delayed space.

I was warned. Now I understood. To take this passage meant to question everything. To upturn and undo every belief I'd ever swallowed. But when I decided to join the Mirage, I knew nothing. Only that my heart was broken and that I'd reached

the firm decision to divert all this love in me,
all this choking love, toward something
benevolent. Something that could absorb
my gifts, my love, take it, use it.

*Please, Someone, feel it, see it, make good with it.
Take it from me, take it out of me, PLEASE.*

Spirit, mind, soul…body…all sore and
broken, restless and yearning. Knowing,
everything, all at once. Although not
knowing anything at all, either. Not a thing.
Just the great mystery of life, which I had
always loved.

ORLA

Arrival of Reverie
Orla. ENTRY №:02

A small group of passengers disembarked the vessel and disappeared into the harbours shadowy thickets. I shivered at the wharfs landing. It was remote. I was remote.
In late afternoon winter light, I awaited the final boat; a small ferry, and the journey to the outer islands. My fingers waivered.

I had come for this fresh air, yet already sought shelter from the cold wind in the humidity of the enclosed passenger lounge, which was more of a tower, a squat lighthouse made of stone sheets of alabaster, limestone and wood.

A frontier outpost, where the heralds and messengers turned around and went back again.

It stood in the wind facing the sun and the racing clouds in still seclusion. Weeping Peppermint trees grew sideways, the driftwood banked at high tide and the jetty was crumbling. A semi-desertion.

The passenger lounge at ground level was a dim cocoon of stillness after the windswept journey. Indistinguishable smiling staff hovered against warm mellow wood-lined walls. Motley benches and seats of past eras and futures, were scattered about. Wide windows faced the ocean, framing a sweeping bay of fluxing boundaries. It made my breath skip.

Low slanting yellow light inched along the back wall of the lounge. The sun was setting West, behind the rolling sea. A sheet of sun-shower slashed on the glass suddenly from a rogue black cloud-squall that swept past the blinding sun, then disintegrated.

I sank down heavily and watched the dust motes swirl in light-shafts upon the stone ground. The mid-winter shadows were at their most spectacular distorted zenith. Plants and old chairs lengthened their limbs in reaching hands of shade.

The cold and shivering in my body eased. The rapid thaw slackened my jaw, and my eyes softened. I could not resist the pink, humid lax light behind closed eyelids and the sound of the sea. For this moment, body and mind seemed in the same place, the spirit settling back in.

I vaguely calculated when the sun would turn back.

Winter Solstice.

Would I turn back too? I sank deeper into the cloying hold of the winged chair and slid into the melt of solar rays penetrating wool… the sensation of heat sinking through to skin. I let it comfort me.

I succumbed to a reverie, the sea hushing…and kind, quiet voices somewhere… A doldrum of suffused thick feeling.

A space opened in my mind to the in-between-places. I recognised it. I'd been here before in dreams and when awake too. I recognised that I need not be who I was before. An old part of me had already rattled free, out there on that Barge, at the river mouth, lost now, blown apart.

To join the Mirage was to start again. It was to leave behind, an other-place, an other-me and transform and so, now…Now. Now…

Now. I walk down shady paths and I seem to know where I am going. Long grasses catch light. The sting still there, still somewhere below or beyond, but not in this focus, not in this soft, soft focus. I make my way down a winding valley road… soft, soft trees, soft, soft grass. Lost shoes. Lost dresses.

Green horizons, gullies of grass. The sound of the sea still there, the smell of frosted-damp-hay sweet in the wind, the sound of softness… soft, soft…so softly… Swaying.

A starry floor on a shining shore.

Was that how it went? The words of the story had invaded my mind. Stars on the earth instead of the sky. Stars above and stars below; the horizon line a knife, a rim of sharp edges, that split everything into two things, and I had a choice to make – above or below? Why always this choice to make? Because you were there, holding gaze. The gaze of ambivalent arrows.

*Take me from this humaneness of humanness.
Take me away from this interminable chasm of
nothing. Let my mind roam free to see the seas edge.
All I want is to feel. Or disappear. Let me*

disappear, let me leave the masses of forgetting… the hasty movements of this rancid, dwindling society…the blindness and waste…the insatiable greed for destruction; the revelling in apocalypse and pestilence… the rummaging apathy… plummeting… warring… subsisting… devouring… haggling to the death…ghouls, half alive, half dead…

Oh god…

An ingratitude slapped me. I recalled wishes ended in cold rooms by guessing faces… dirty floors slept on, rotting tunnels fallen in, years of hitch-sail. The lack of grace, the sharp sensitivity. False self-disclosure, false friends ready to destroy the first scrap of evidence of hard-earned self-worth…*don't shine, don't thrive, don't dream, hide your talent, hold your tongue….*

Get me to the Island. That is NOT MY VOICE.

I'd been warned of this – that the closer I got to the Ferry, the more I might dissolve.

That parts of me that didn't belong, that were false and destructive, would emerge raw then fall away. That I'd have to plan for re-birth. That there would be confusion and a sense of loss. Right now, I had a loss of orientation.

Shadows crossed halls…

Just dreams.

I awoke to a room without sun or sound, and wondered if I'd managed to sleep through an invitation which I knew would never, ever-ever, come again.

So suddenly then, I leapt up! Grabbing my luggage in such a swift movement and racing out the door so fast that I realised my body had made the decision for me and I was thankful. A spirit had awoken me!

My spirit!

Yes!

I was going! I was running…A force had lifted me…propelled this body of flaws….I ran as fast as I could, waving to something below; a light!… I could see only dim twilight and shadows below, perhaps a rocking lantern.

Run!…

The relief at seeing the dusky outline of the small vessel still roped to the wharf was effervescent, another swathe of excitement – an impetuous *Yes!* A surge of momentum through my chest; a physical symptom of joy, so right, so clear, a buoyant lack of friction, a choice I trusted with glee!

Lasers….of thoughts flickered through me as I scrambled down the twi-lit cliff, the sea mist had thickened in the winter air, sucking down to earth in velvet-vapour of deepest grey. I waved again to the Bailiff's square shoulders in the fading light and ran gracelessly…

Did I leave something behind?

So quickly did I descend to enter the vessel, so fast was that motion, so final was my seated position at the low rear starboard, that my peripheral vision seemed to have evaporated. I could not see either side of me, no matter how hard I looked and only the pinpoint of my frontal vision was in focus. How this occurred I do not know, I had managed to board the Ferry, yet not having noticed what it looked like, only the Bailiff's calm expression and his hand urging me on.

No-one could answer my questions, no one could hear me, I could scarcely see them, so could they see me? The Bailiff had been so re-assuring. I simply closed hazy eyes and waited, as the only thing that would really come into focus now were the 'M' creases on the palms of my hands.

Even they seemed to be moving, waiting to be directed, waiting for a new incision, a new formation, a re-arrangement of the same things in a new way. I tried hard to remember, to memorise the palm lines, but they kept moving. Would this heart ache be gone too by the time I arrived? Suddenly it was searing again.

A fleshly-felt-stabbing gash struck into a beating belly, twinging through to my lungs. *Do I really want to forget?* Too late, too late… and still not knowing what side of the knife I would land upon, I willed my mind to be at peace and listened to the sound of the hull sliced by sea.

And then I awoke. Still in the doldrum sunrays of the passenger lounge tower, awaiting the ferry to the island. I'd only been asleep for minutes and felt disorientated, clotted with strange intuitions and ….those… *laser-quick*…thoughts in my dream…*flashed.*

I pulled my notebook from my bag and flipped with eyes half closed, remembering, …feeling…uneasy, holding the pencil, ready to scribe it down, then anxious as the image faded.

A message, an omen?....Something at the edge would not come back and the vision evaporated.

I caressed my notebook, the texture of paper soothing, the cover faded and seasoned. I pulled out the ancient, tattered pages I'd wedged in, unfolded and re-folded a thousand times, my coveted acquisition, or at least the fragments of it trusted to my possession. *'Isle of the Mirage'*, a description of events, perhaps a legend, written by some poetess of the future for me now, in the past.

PROLOGUE

Those who lived close-by to the Isle, may have heard tales, but the evidence was scanty at the time of writing circa 5270's A.D.II. (After 2nd Deluge).

This translation is the only known written account of the Sanctuary of the Mirage Isle and the souls that lived there in its final days.

It may be of interest to people of the past, that are still be-coming, so that they may recognise it when it comes.

✠ *Also known simply as 'The Mirage'; the Adepts who lived in the Sea Caves in the last inhabitable occupied Isles of Old Earth before the 3rd Deluge.*

CHAPTER ONE
Isle of the Mirage

I n a distant time, a Mirage of women live secluded on an Islet by the Deep Green Sea. They live beyond the veil of customary sight, far away in the remotest part of the Southern Antipodes, in a region inconceivable and therefore invisible, to most.

For those who do arrive, the first thing noticed is the appearance of contrasts; a polarity of light which creates a peculiar luminosity amid dark shadows. Inky night skies mirror stars onto gleaming, shining shores. The seaweed sings in rustling whispers and the shells have eyes.

Upon this island, pure springs erupt from underground, first hot, then tepid, then running cool over rocks, fresh and vital.

Plentiful orchards overflow with fruit and berries, and animals, birds and fish teem in thousands.

Souls of the lost, the fragmented or bewildered, often find the Isle, for their hearts are scoured. A matriarchy governs the Isle, welcoming shipwrecked beings; the broken and searching ones, favourable to the Mirage's cause, ready to be rebuilt.

These souls have opened the door to the pre-birth and post-death of life and their lack of fear reveals to them the mysteries the Isle offers. They arrive like hollow wicker and dry grass and become strong again by listening and remembering.

The realms boundary, mirror-like and alive, can also be slipped through by clever creatures, men and women, perhaps accidently while dreaming or dozing or dying, or intentionally by those who have woken up, or figured out how to cross through the mirror, but it is rare, and few wanderers live on the island.

Shifting divisions of space and time form partitions to other spaces and difficult-to-name places and times, so one must be ready to navigate. It is essential to stay in a particular frequency, so not surprisingly then, disappearances are rife, but the sepulchre is empty. Souls simply vanish.

The seven senior Mirage Anchorites; *Those-Whom-Never-Leave*, have for millennia the sole vocation of tender custody of the transcendent laws of the Absolute. All wisdom and divine knowledge of the infinite void is preserved for a future age. A holding-over, to tide humanity through the dark age of its next evolutionary leap. The mathematics of the universe, gene keys and codes, the language of source. Equations of light.

The Mirage women have carefully gathered wisdom lost to cyclic millennia of floods, fires and freezes on Gaia. It was often said upon the Isle; 'Who knows what the tide will fetch today?'.

Their mission is to ensure consciousness continues to expand and evolve in human form. Salvaged manuscripts and oral traditions are distilled; divinity is chronicled into lectionaries of script, diagrams and epithets.

The fledgling young Mirage Acolytes; *Those-in-Learning,* arrive often wrapped just in rags. Great sacrifices are demanded well before even reaching the Isle and to join the Sanctuary as Acolyte is a privileged attainment that may take a lifetime to realise.

Acolytes begin with chants to drum in knowledge to body-memory with song and dance. Tattoos are given in contemplation of chosen disciplines. Scribes and artists carefully replicate texts and draw from stories told by wanderers. The bodies of the senior Mirage, the Adepts; *Those-Whom-Hold,* become, over time, living, moving libraries of knowledge, keepers in organic form, of the undeniable laws of the cosmos.

As above so below.

The Isle, the last of the sacred world on Earth, the rest now putrid, has kept the world from being entirely cast adrift, by a thin veil, just a few silken mirror threads, just hanging on delicately, in space.

A life-raft-in-waiting, the women observe the invisible rhythms of creation. They are guards, protecting a treasure, conductors composing currents of energy, weaving everyday a harmony of light within themselves and without, which must remain at all times, resolutely in tune.

The Mirage women are mediators between sacred and secular. They await the next diluvian age of flood. They know the signs of its coming. And they dream of the victorious sail to New Earth.

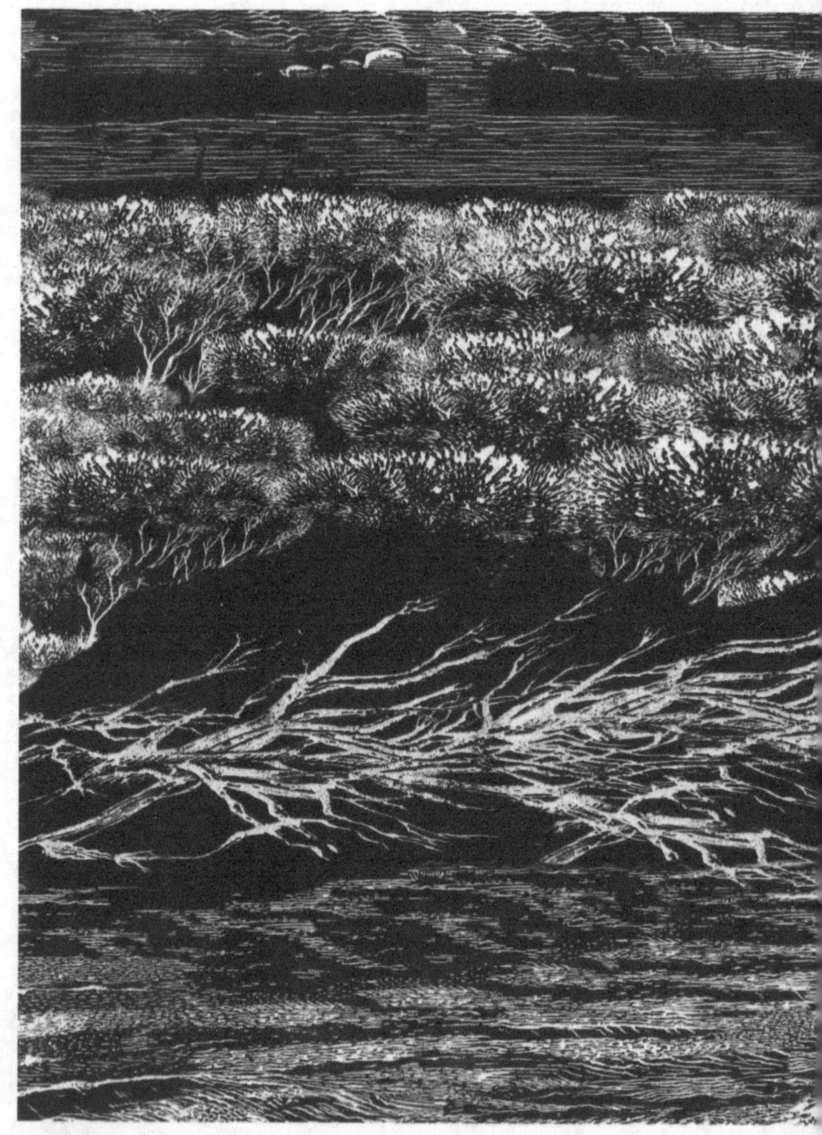

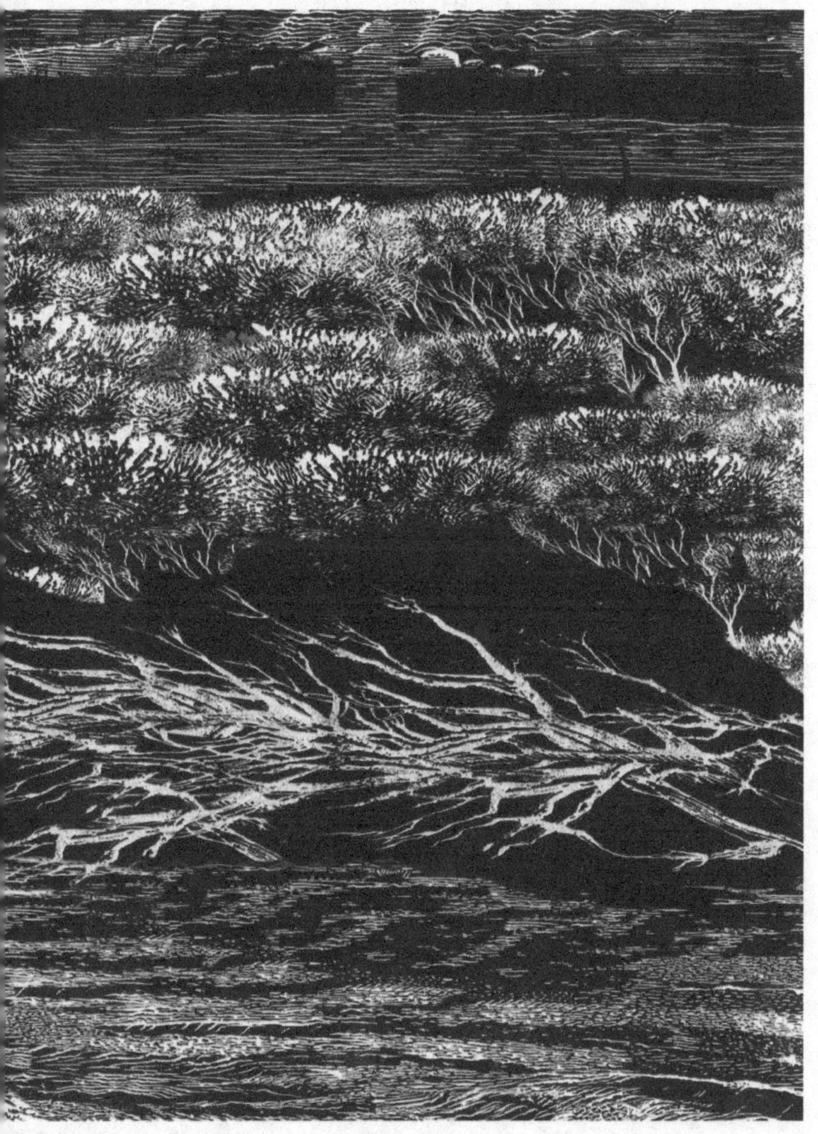

CHAPTER TWO
The Fisherman and the Selkie

There was a Fisherman, who lived along the isolated coast on the outskirts of the Mirage's boundary. His disposition meant that he had glimpsed the Mirage Isle from time to time and sensed that the legends must be true. But he had no desire to attempt passage. He was happy to catch his fish, trace his traditions and live far from the fraying chaos of the dying world.

He had married a Selkie woman, whose people had returned to life in the sea after the last diluvian age. The Selkie merrily forfeited her sealskin to him but had become restless with the Fisherman's long days at sea, and now desperately wanted to have a child.

The Fisherman loved the Selkie with all his heart, even when she was cold and distant and stared at the sea for hours silent and withdrawn. He found himself by day in a semi-prayer to the sky, bidding for a child to come.

One evening, while yanking nets at the tide line, a soft ripple of sea caught his attention. A giant Bishop-Fish, standing tall by tail in the shallow water, with fins held wide, looked him straight in the eye and exclaimed:

"Fisherman! I have heard your wish that a child of your loins should be birthed of your Selkie wife, and it may come true, but it will come at a cost".

"It is all I've wanted Bishop-Fish. Tell me, please!? What must I do?"

"Fisherman, you must take splendid gifts to the seven Mirage High Priestesses – they are the Anchorites; the self-exiled women who live and toil in the sea caves nearby – seven gifts, no more, no less. And…"

"Yes, Bishop-Fish, we have many treasures retrieved from the sea by my wife and I'm prepared to pay the price."

"Ah, but I had not finished dear Fisherman, you will indeed be blessed with a child, but you must always remember that there is the possibility that the child may be taken from you some-day…"

Some-day…That seemed very far away to the Fisherman, and he pondered the look of joy in his wife's eyes when she saw her belly swell with a child and so he said:

"I accept, good Bishop-Fish, I accept, and I will prepare the gifts and deliver them to the Mirage as you say."

"Fisherman, you and your wife will be met here at dawn – do not be late!" And the Bishop-Fish disappeared under the waves.

The couple prepared the seven gifts for the Mirage. The Selkie wife examined her collection of treasures recovered from the sea floor and arranged seven giant glass jars to fill with the most useful and beautiful materials of barter in the region.

She filled one jar with sand dollars for grinding fine mortar into white paint, another she filled with large sharks' teeth – the kind that are effective in tools and medicine, another with urchin skeletons that make the purples and greens and blues for dyeing cloth. A fourth jar was filled with green-black pearls for games and amusement. A fifth jar was filled with lightning whelks whose sound to the ear was of thunder and high-seas and the voices of loved ones, favourable to travellers who must leave the coast. A sixth jar was filled with rare deep-sea golden sea-wrack, whose fibrous tendrils held medicine so powerful it healed almost any ailment.

Finding nothing else of value among her hoard, the Selkie decided the only other thing worthy of the Mirage, would be the bullion-gold mirror she had found in a dissolving shipwreck that had lain on the seabed for many thousands of years. What use a mirror might be to these secluded women she did not know, but it was all she had, apart from useless gold coins which the Mirage did not value or use. The seven gifts were arranged, and the couple slept in peace.

At dawn as promised, a group of young novices, the Acolytes; *Those-in-Becoming*, met the Fisherman and the Selkie on the winter shore, along with the Bailiff who was among the few dozen men living on the Island.

Selected by fate, these men had arrived like many others, but stayed on long enough, without disappearing, to establish their frequency of support, protection and allegiance to the Mirage Sanctuary.

The small group boarded a sturdy skiff whose wooden prow was carved with ornate symbols of crosses and flowering seagrasses. The Bailiff told the newcomers that the cross symbolised 'As above, so below' and the flowering grasses signified 'Life Eternal' and that the men of the Isle carved them for the women as a gift.

The voyage was short, for it seemed they only left their bay of bleached sand and fishing nets and returned to the same one, but the rock formations were slightly odd, as if they had a lively echo. The shadows were deeper, the light phosphorescent.

The tender-footed Acolytes led the Fisherman and the Selkie along the beach toward distant cliffs, then through a bewildering maze of twists and turns in mountains and valleys of rock, where spiky grasses and malleable vines covered every surface.

It seemed they were heading to the middle of the island, but in a disorientating interval, they stepped out of a windless coastal garden and walked for some time on another secluded beach where more islets lay just offshore, across sheltered lagoons so green and glass-clear that even the Selkie gasped in disbelief.

The Bailiff disappeared down an over-grown path, but the Selkie and the Fisherman continued to follow the young Acolytes who summoned them onwards. Eventually, after quite some time more, they rounded another high rocky cliff and entered a shady wood. Rocky caves along the escarpment, looked inhabited and inviting, glowing with soft-warm flickers in sheltered clearings.

The wood became denser still and light became limited, but speckled, dappled beams shone through in patches upon the ground. The ocean roared loud above all sounds. They edged a swamp that indicated a recent high neep tide. The smell of the earth and sea was rich, sweet and fresh.

Finally, they were ushered into one of the many caves and furtively down a spiral of stairs carved into black basalt and peacock ore that shimmered even in the dimness.

A labyrinth of dark passages, solid tunnels of rock, as cool as the bottom of the ocean, delivered them finally into a cavernous, concealed sea grotto. In its centre was a large moon pool filled with the trembling light of the sky and bouncing illuminations. The pool cave was surrounded by smooth ancient tamala limestone and weathered hexagons of volcanic basalt. The ceiling glittered with fireflies; a luminescent gathering on stone over-head. A powerhouse and a house of power with a slim chute to the sky far above. It was the Cardinal Sea Cathedral of the Mirage.

Upon seven hexagons of basalt, sat the seven senior Mirage Anchorite's; *Those-Whom-Never-Leave*. The women wore the most remarkable clothing which appeared weathered, tattered, worn and washed and dyed and repaired a thousand times; the rescued scraps woven with the simple magic of old technology into wondrous cascades of shape and form, faded colour and intricate pattern.

A delightful music tinkled, breathing in and out with the wind and the tide, just lightly tapping on rock, a pitter-patter percussion. The sound echoed and rippled around the cave in radiant colour and seaweed drifting at the edges of the moon pool swayed in-time, releasing tiny bubbles in pure euphonic harmony. A vaporous song expelled, sucking and heaving in time to the slow surge of sea. This place it seemed, had a natural synaesthesia; colours with sound and sound that was coloured.

The women rose in sequence and performed a dance that seemed entirely for themselves, slowly pirouetting with some invisible force. A communion of sorts.

As the dance ceased and the Mirage sat down again, it appeared timely for the Fisherman and the Selkie, who stood bewildered by the token of the dance, to lay down their seven gifts at the feet of each

Priestess. The Fisherman spoke, quietly but firmly.

"Thank you, High Priestesses, Revered Senior Anchorites of the Isle of Mirage, for your dance, and for receiving us in your most sacred place. We bring gifts, as the Bishop-Fish told us you may be able to grant our wish to conceive a child".

"We know of your wish, and we thank you for these gifts…." They all seemed to speak as if in vibration, all at once… "We grant your wish, and in return we will bestow seven wishes for the new child, ready to be conceived."

The Fisherman and the Selkie gave each other a longing look of loves promise, then each woman spoke to the couple in turn.

The first High Priestess, a navigator, astrologer and scientist, vowed that the child would arrive in one year. The second, the foremost Healer on the Isle promised that "the child will have health, strength and merit;

toiling well by day and sleeping in peace by night."

The third High-Priestess who was a teacher, archivist and librarian, assured the child would have keen instincts and a mysterious wisdom from the time the eyes first opened.

The fourth High Priestess, sitting in the centre as Abbattissa; *Ministerial-Mother* who led the devotions and sanctified the Cathedral, smiled upon the couple and pledged that the child would have the favour and indulgence of the Mirage forever more.

The Fisherman realised that this was a significant transaction, one that he may regret, but it was far too late to turn back.

The fifth High Priestess, the Orchard Guardian and a Master Calligrapher, pronounced solemnly and simply that the child carried an extraordinary fate.

The sixth High Priestess, the Mirage Sybil, an old weaver, who had been in position as

High Priestess for over 300 years now, stood suddenly in a kind of trance, divination leaves strewn at her feet, an elixir fresh in her veins…her eyes glazed with black rim she spoke dazzlingly;

"This child to come will sail the Ark Coracle when the waves come…the child will raise a vault of flutes…and nets of…knowledge…" The Sybil reached blindly ahead, looking for her vision…Her sight waivered, but then she saw again, a *flash*…

"…Nets and Vaults…Flutes! of light…that will realise… an eternal Sanctuary for all…" she repeated again, "The child will sail the Ark Coracle…." She then collapsed back upon her basalt perch as if spent of all energy.

The Fisherman and the Selkie's eyes grew wider and wider with each utterance. It was as if each Mirage member must out-do the previous bestowment, as if each sister of this hidden lair must exceed in extravagance and grandeur, the promise of the one before!

The seventh and longest serving of the current Mirage High Priestesses, the Adoratrice; *Keeper-of-the-Keys*, who saw that her gift was the gold mirror, was agitated at the other Mirage members for granting upon the yet-to-be-born child such great destiny, so she exclaimed:

"That may be so! But this child will also be cursed with endless trials and lose these gifts! Every one of them she will lose before her time is done!"

The remaining Mirage collectively gaped in disbelief at the unexpected eruption of churlish venom from the Key Keeper, but the spell had ended its reckoning and nothing further could be done.

The Fisherman and the Selkie were escorted back across to their coastal home by the Bailiff and the young Acolytes, all the while rejoicing affectionately that in the next three months they would conceive. They had no other wish than to have a child, so to be promised so many gifts only to then have them withdrawn meant little to them. Their child was coming.

The Fisherman had not told the Selkie of the Bishop-Fish's dire warning that the child may be taken away, but he did not have the heart to break her happiness.

The In-between
Orla. ENTRY №:03

Gladly would I have stayed in the tower. In that passenger lounge. In that warm place of in-between. It kept the grief and hope in equilibrium, buoyant in space it seemed, like a holding of breath. The ticking clock and ocean hushing held everything in suspended momentum, like a sea-train. It forced one within, to disconnect from the before and after.

The paradox at the still centre of this seesaw in time, was that change was pregnant in every atom. Staying was unviable, and this tension pushed in all directions, imposing a timeless vacancy.

If I were to make it to the island, to join the Mirage, then I needed to focus. *Centre.* Behind eyelids. Undo every-thing I ever knew. Breathe. Ask. Wait. See. One eye within, one eye without. Go in and down, within.

Listen.

Dropping into the edge-less awareness, I travelled gently but quickly back across territories and asked to see again the giant cinema screen, set in the sky, large enough to make impact. I asked for an even bigger picture.

Let me see....

Flashing cycles in sequence of 12,000 Earth years pass, again and again. Mere micro-seconds on the celestial scale.

The planet re-births in afterglow light. Another cycle.... An almost-Eden emerges from ruin then sabotages straight into self-extinction. Satellites crash, remaining life scurries underground.

The process starts again in the Earth's core. An invisible seismic rattle in deep and far space swelling in patterns of electro-magnetic energy… a small, slow ripple moving within an immeasurably vast universe…the gravitational force of nearby planets sparking…accelerating… A localised flurry of nothingness, when perceived within the eternally expanding conscious orb of quantum fluctuation in every direction. But an unanswerable cataclysm for Gaian's.

Explosions of magma blister out across the globe, cracking through here, there, first streams, then rivers of steaming water and lava. Valleys fold along fault-lines, swallowing whole peaks. A black rivulet of fire melts the poles…the water levels rise rapidly for days…tides start to suck in and out…revealing the Pacific Ocean plate and sunken cities, then flooding, colossal crashing tsunami, then the sky turns black, spreading, seeping, cooling, smothering the lithosphere.

It takes hundreds of years for the sky to clear, and hundreds for the ice to melt. Hundreds of years to unearth submerged cities and collect debris on remote shores…

What would survive this time? And Who?

And all the while, still, a glowing light… The light first. The light before the dark. *The light came first.* For without light, there cannot be dark…

The time to catch the ferry to the Mirage Isle was nearly here. This time I would make it. The cut-out doll eyes of self, opened in my notebook, and I sought the familiar diversion of tales and constancies, to sooth my inner disquiet.

CHAPTER THREE
The Birth and the Death

One year later, on a rare Earth morning, winter sun sent a pale glow down to the world. A mist had arisen out at sea in the night and settled thickly in strange shapes over rocky forms along the beach. Foggy shafts of light travelled down damply, piercing gold through cloud vapour.

A rumbling unearthly phosphorescence lingered over the sand, creating a sense of impending deliverance and the Selkie mother knew it was time to bare down and birth the child. She asked the Fisherman for her sealskin so that the child might be born of the sea without pain.

The Selkie witnessed the unsettling aura of pre-sentiment. The seabirds were shrieking in erratic lifts and dives and the fish flicked close to shore, circling in a primitive dance under lulls of quiet breakers. As the low dawn sun climbed behind the shadow of Earth and thunder cloud, a dimness re-descended and a million eerie shades of indigo suspended momentarily on the horizon, stirring every creature with a further rush of restless, unnameable longing.

Then, under a sharp breast of broken escarpment, in a cold sea cave, the seal-child was born. Dead. The child was dead-blue. The Selkie mother could see that the child had the rare condition where its seal fur was inside out and separate to the body, like an external organ that hung attached only at the nape of the neck like a loose cape. Or in this case, a noose, that had strangled the child.

The Selkie mother was so startled by the sight, that she became immediately full of fear, dread and sadness. She peered at her child's white face and its blue-ish, pink-ish mottled limbs. It's large black dead-still-imploring eyes kept the mother in the cave for only a momentary sniff and wriggle before she departed hastily with shame and distress twitching at her nose.

The poor Selkie mother wondered why the Bishop-Fish ever made such oaths, and why the Mirage had made such promises if only to break them cruelly. She tumbled into the sea and disappeared.

The child had only slipped over the veil by moments, just enough to pierce the threshold and cross over to the Mirage Isle. The child hovered between two worlds.

Suddenly awakening, it sensed the danger of being abandoned so completely and understanding instinctively the aggrieved departing dive of the mother, the child rolled into its own fur and decided it would do all it could to live, all it could do to survive.

The pouchy-oil-musk of seal-birthing, aroused the young Sea Wolf who roamed the dark capes of the Islet cliffs. Hungry for days and alone, the Wolf paced down through the clashing chasms and tiers of rock, seeking out the earthy salt-blood-balm.

The fishy mammalian pungency of wet fur and congealed blood roused the Wolfs hunger unfathomable. His lust for game insatiable. With his in-breath burning, he carefully concealed himself, wary of the Mirage of women who dwelled close-by who did not understand his shadowy-shaman ways of criss-crossing the veil.

The strange light of the sky was like an omen of purpose that propelled the Wolf toward his meal. He too, felt the strange disquieting ambience upon the shore and paced quickly past the all-seeing-shell-eyes that washed up daily upon his shore. He ignored their implored imperious reproach of soundless words and leapt hastily into the cave, ready to devour the baby seal, already licking his lips for the taste of sweet flesh.

What shock was his, to find this saline covered creature; alert, with an unflinching stare and whiskers sprouting from a plump, smooth and well-formed face. When the Wolf licked a slow pulse and smiled down with his snaggle tooth bite upon her limb, the seal-child turned its eyes in tender trust toward the beast, reaching out for his ears, pulling him closer.

In great shock the Wolf sprang back! In that same jolting moment of puzzling sensation, the Wolf and the seal exchanged a glance that held time and a thousand words, but the walking-bells of the Mirage arrived vibrant and brassy above the sound of rolling surf and the Wolf leapt out of the cave so quickly he could not tell what had startled him more!

From the safety of a craggy shaft of sea rock, the Wolf watched the young Mirage Acolytes make their approach. Their trailing shrouds and mantles moved absurdly slow.

The procession lingered to salvage a tidal offering, then a sudden cacophony of white veils and high shrieking erupted as they neared the birth cave.

"A child is upon the rock!", a shout and collective gasps of astonishment, "O!...Who left her here!?"...."Where is her Mother!?".....

"Where is her Father!?"....

"Abandoned?!"

The women gathered quickly around the child, huddling into the mouth of the dim rookery, crouching over to see if the child was asleep or dead. The Mirage bells softened yet continued, absorbing the solemn moment into the morning ritual. Voices lowered as they encircled the child and observed the inexplicable and bloody scene. "Look the placenta still beats! Look it's moving!" an urgent whisper.

The women witnessed the pink, purple and blue of the engorged birth caul, as it gaped and puckered over the rocks, moving, pulsing, grunting with fresh plasma through to the child's omphalos, its centre. The Wolf's paw leaping upon it had resuscitated the babe further, pumping fresh blood into veins, so despite the smears of blood and salt covering the child, it seemed settled and slumbered, burrowing down its transparent silver-white skin into the warm pelted fur splayed under its flanks.

The bells continued softly brimming in the hand of a young Acolyte.

"Oh! But this child, this beautiful child!...." in hushes now....and with pity...

"Oh, this child, look at its feet and look at its hands..." in awe and quiet and sorrow now...

Tucked into the coppery fur that appeared joined at its neck in a thick fold of skin and creases of blubber, the child's hands and feet were flipper-like, paws not human or seal, but almost lupine, of a soft white-grey, with sharp talons at the tip of each webbed phalange. Clutched in one paw tightly was a large piece of broken shell, mostly obscured by fur and blood and sand and muck.

The Mirage reached forward and gently touched the child-animal, with a generous amount of love and care. A rag mantle was wrapped over and carefully tucked under the seal skin cape, softly. But suddenly fresh bright blood appeared in a quick widening circle upon the cloth, oozing, flowing freely, a rivulet of blood pouring, purple, gushing.

"This blood is still fresh….Oh, Oh! She is injured! Look here at these puncture wounds!" a shred of gasps now…

"Oh my! Oh, she is struggling!!"

The Mirage's exclamations lulled and hushed to a chanting hymn of supplication. The child closed its eyes peacefully and with a rapid loss of its pink flush, began to turn blue before the Mirage's eyes. The placenta stilled again its slow pulse, and the Mirage bells ceased too. The women looked to each other with their knowing eyes and hearts of sound-council and with all the shifting haste and strife of that eerie and restless morning, they simply sat and sang and beheld the miraculous, woeful creature.

The young Wolf, who had watched on, still in shock at the familiar embrace of the strange seal-pup and its calm dark eyes, bounded away to his shadowy cliff filled with baby seal bones, a feeling of loss in his heart rather than his stomach, and with a long hollow howl he ran far away, deep into shrouded thickets.

The all-seeing-shell-eyes upon the shore merely blinked, for they had seen this all before.

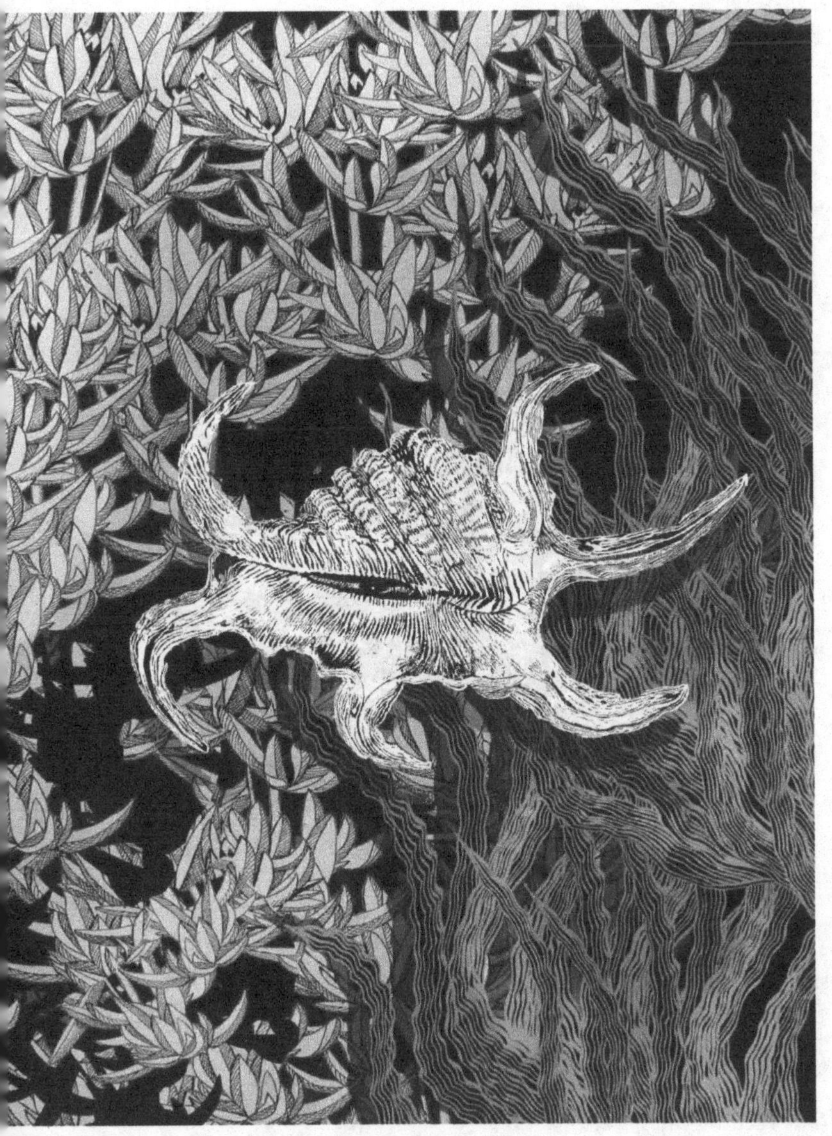

CHAPTER FOUR

Descent to the Underworld

A Mirage Acolyte rushed the child to the sanatorium where the High Priestess of Healing dwelled beside natural springs of warm water. Suddenly the Bishop-Fish appeared in the sea-spring and spoke in a clear voice.

"This is the child of the Selkie and the Fisherman. Her name is Roe, after the orange of the scallop that is in her grandfathers' hair. Keep her safe."

The Bishop Fish touched the babe on the forehead, whispered something in her ear and descended back in the water. Roe was limp and lifeless, a dead weight in the Mirages' arms. Her eyes stared blankly outward, dull, and glazed. She was still wrapped in cloth and dripping with blood, and the placenta, although still attached, had ceased its miraculous surges.

The Healer did all she could with her therapies and care, but still, the child did not awake. Plied from Roe's cold grip the Priestesses took the piece of broken shell, only to find it a human-like jawbone, still with a golden tooth wedged in the mandible. It was cleaned and returned to Roe's webbed fingers. The umbilical cord and placenta were removed and stored in a jar.

From where she was laid on warm stone, Roe hovered the periphery of death, submitting to a sinking feeling that somehow allowed her whole body to dissolve, like a melting of grains of sand downwards, but then floating up, instead of down, she felt her whole body, every atom going through this process, this slipping, squeezing, going through the eye, backwards, down but forwards and up all at the same time. It was a feeling of becoming entirely small and into nothing, as well as enlarging outside her skin and fur, pushing out, bursting out. The sensation was entirely strange, yet with little experience of life to go by, she surrendered to the sensation curiously and felt into its numbness.

The mumbling sounds of the Bishop-Fish in her ear, hardly detected when given, seemed to somehow arrange and come to life in her mind. Clear messages came instantly, a wealth of knowledge, all at once, all that is, all known things, crystallised firmly in her minds' eye.

Becoming aware however, that she could not move, a fear began to prickle and roam her skin, a still shiver that could not be expressed, a vice-like grip then began to squeeze her, a suffocating, disorientating, frozen choke. Her limbs would not move, her whole body became petrified and stiff, locked-up, heavy upon the stone. Her bark was mute, her tongue rolled to the back of her throat and then too, her eyes turned inwards and looked into her mind. Even more fearsome sights and sensations then descended upon her. Fear set in with pain and pricklings. Strange creatures wandered in a procession to torture her, each new one performing some awful demonstration expertly with knives and pins and ugly hands and mouthless faces. They spread her legs and needled her womb, over and over. They filled her with liquids, stoppered her with corks then squeezed her until she almost burst. They poked and prodded and slashed and stitched her.

Eventually in blackness she could no longer detect anything outside herself. Within, she endured an endless measure of terrifying pain. Minutes, hours, days, weeks and then months passed, the same thing continued, repeating over and over, a never ceasing endless dread.

The Selkie drifted in this underworld. An awareness of herself lying on the stone returned and the cave seemed like an aquarium of dark and light shades, and she drifted between the two.

Occasionally when the pain and fear and shuddering of her small body became too much, a light would appear and how she longed to move toward its softness. A kind of peace would accompany the light, and she saw gentle creatures, manta rays, dolphins and whales slowly swimming in light, her tail and flippers were able to move again, and she was free! Her Selkie skin fit snug and water-tight and she sensed that finally she was going home.

No sooner had she started the long swim with the sea creatures when suddenly the light disappeared and again, she found herself trapped in another cave. This one darker, dimmer, colder and more petrifying.

A new procession of faces appeared, they spoke without moving their lips and their eyes were dead and sorry for her mute-freeze, and she turned to the stone she laid upon. Becoming part of the cave floor, cold, lifeless and passive. Her eyes opened but without a body to move, she stared at the same vision, the sound of ocean somewhere...

Nothing noticed her, she became invisible, living inside rock, things began to grow on her, more weeks passed and seaweed began to attach itself to her limbs, and grow in her eyes. Crabs took up residence in every fold and crevice, little fishes nibbled at her ears and toes, tickling and itching yet she could not reach for them, and this felt as distressful as the pins and knives of the mouthless creatures that continued to stream past her, taking their turn to find some new way to weaken her.

A hunger gnawed at her insides like a hollow echo and her parched mouth ached for sustenance. Memories of the safe womb of formation occasionally returned; the gurgling and roar and hush of the ocean and a mothers' heartbeat. A slow stirring brought a memory of the eternal splitting and growing of the soul as it came down the star-path and the dive into the whirl of cells and nerves expanding and contracting... This blissful escape raised hopes...but then she would fall back again, into the agony of her rock-tomb self.

The Blinking Passage
Orla. ENTRY №:04

The sun lowered and it was finally time to board the lantern-lined Ferry. The scene struck odd, Antipodean, a foreign and exotic upside world of tropical-gothic-Oceania in dry shade. The sky outlined with mysterious faunas, spiky grasses and flowers inhospitable, dreadful in their beauty.

I marvelled that I was the only passenger. The Bailiff looked sourly at my luggage.

"Leave everything behind."

"Everything?"

"It will be here when you return"

"But I don't plan on coming back."

"Regardless, if you are ready to depart, the luggage must stay. Please leave it there and come aboard, we embark immediately".

He watched me step down into the narrow prow. I looked at my black case left on the Jetty. Now it was just the clothes on my back. And the notebook in my jacket pocket. I knew I should leave it. But the Ferryman had thrown the rope. We were leaving and the decision was made for me.

We pushed off into the tide silently. The Bailiff watched me from behind. I felt exposed. That stirring feeling came back. The movement of an onward-ness swelling as we joined the tide. I began to let myself believe I was finally on my way…Hope beyond the horizon…Clean air, clean wind, salty sea.

We were now halfway to the Islet and as it came into view, I marvelled that it was so close. That I had come so far. My eyes closed to thank my guides, but quickly

opened again to hungrily drink in the vision
of the unspoilt island as we drew near. Its
tiers and waterfalls in the low light, its grassy
expanses wavering, its perfect white sand.
Its promise of noble labour.

Light emanated and absorbed all at once
across the bluffs and bays. The clouds were
white fire. I turned smiling to the Bailiff, but
he was shaking his head. Within a blink I
was back again. Back in the passenger
lounge wing chair.

No! I raced passed the fluxing
windows…down to the pier, the Jetty was
still crumbling, the Ferry still awaited, but
the Bailiff was nowhere to be seen. My
luggage was not where he said it would be.
It was just me and the clothes on my back
and the notebook.

Why can't I cross over? I'm ready!

I walked back toward the tower and the
departure lounge. The beaches were still
deserted, the pathways shadowy, the wind

strong and crisp. A man appeared on the path facing me. He casually stopped and rested upon the Jetty's crumbling steps, looking out to sea, appearing as if he awaited my approach. He seemed sage and had warm laughing eyes.

"You realise don't you, that you have to leave it all behind?" he said it so lovingly, with a laugh, chuckling, a knowingness that let me know he thought I could do it.

"Go now, down to the sea behind the other side of the tower. It will feel like you are being torn apart, but you are just expanding. Let yourself out." He smiled again, so warmly. He seemed layered somehow. Stacked with depth. Familiar.

He nodded toward the beach and handed me a box of matches. I smiled and thanked him, my cheeks flaring red. As soon as he was behind me, I felt his eyes on my back and I wanted to hide from all gazes, to enclose myself away, to be hidden. To get this work done. I immediately regretted not engaging with him further and realised it was partially my pride in appearing proficient that could be thwarting this passage.

Ask for help. You must ask.

Descending the trail to the back beach, I found a rocky nook to pause from the wind amongst driftwood, coastal plants and seashells, where the sand lay untrodden and squeaky clean. It was far enough from the tower to be private. The sea rolled in fresh and hushing. Somehow the beauty brimmed into clear eyes, returning the calling unrest that sent my awareness to the hundred shades of cloud on the horizon again…

A magnet of disquiet? *No.* Or a sign of never-ending energy lines to follow? *Yes.*

The invisible brick in the belly tugged, dragging dark blood through to the heart, charging my spine with seizures once again.

Beyond these symptoms, there was only one way through. *Step aside and witness.*

Surrender. It was impossible to swallow or push aside. I allowed the withering… sinking… falling to knees. Clenching the sand between fingers and toes, a chasm opened and with it the realisation of how much there was still to shed.

Please No. The head sunk.

Another roll…an internal wave of shaking descent… down through the frame to the pit, the root, and beyond, began again. Again and again, over and over, waves of fire and ice, tingling, burning, the spine expanding, brain twitching. I veered from the sensations grip, but it had me. I willed it away, but it grew, and held, and grew and became a glow that almost felt…*Euphoric.*

Pain or pleasure? The cosmic wave. Which came… *overcome.* It overcame me. My whole body expanded to fit this new spirit. The growing hurt. As the vapours expelled from my mouth in dark foams and gels, a light filled me from below, saving self from shattering.

The clamping freeze swelled, hovering before shutdown. Knuckles spread white gripping sand. The stomach threshed and clenched and rolled. Neck muscles fossilised, kinking, setting like lead and terrible gasps escaped in pace with the seizing collapse. On and on, the keening song returned and droned.

Does it ever end? This purging?

How many have come here? How many have left it all behind here on this beach? A switch was taking place.

It's not a knowing. It's an upgrade of becoming. To transform takes metamorphosis. It cannot be learnt, only experienced.

My faith quivered. I stood and spun around under the enormous sky. *Must I leave it all?* All I had was the notebook of lessons, diary entries, letters; the words that made my heart light up. My name written in the notebook seemed absurd and distant, my past vague, valuable and void. Still, I sat upon the knifes edge.   The horizon line loomed, cutting the world in half.

A reversal. A walk-in of *other*. I can't take any of this? *No.* I knew the answer. The notebook and tattered pages of the Mirage Isle folktale I'd carried for years was again under my fingers…I was so attached to its accounts of arrival and departure. *Take nothing with you.* No need. I knew the story by heart.

CHAPTER FIVE
Labyrinth of Dark and Light

Roe's pain had gone, but she still could not move. She could hear the splashes of Mirage women and echoes of light on the cave roof, which now she saw in very close detail. Something else now though, with this sinking and expanding feeling. A dizziness, and fizziness. As if she had lifted to the roof even as she sank below the ground. She realised suddenly that she could see from every angle, every point in the cavernous grotto-cathedral, so, even though she couldn't move, and her eyes were closed, she was able to explore.

The Bishop-Fish spoke in her mind in a language she understood, it was as if when the fish-mouth opened, a stream of musical tones and messages sunk through to her, saying one word but delivering immense knowledge. So much time had passed, but none at all.

The whispering, whispering of the Bishop-Fish went on, and Roe kept learning. Others were there to teach her too, other fish and seals and even the seaweed waved and sighed a joyful devotion. The shell-eyes telepathed. She felt love then and understood unconditional love.

She heard music that caused joyful waves to swell her heart. A thousand-fold magnification of harmonies that brimmed…an overflowing cascade of delightful sensations that landed in and on her skin, into her eyes and through her chest. The dazzling light flickering on the cave ceiling rose up and up and up and opened in blazing brightness that should have burnt her eyes, but instead was stardust softness, delightful and warm. She rose up higher to meet the stars and saw the dark of the night sky outside and distant galaxies twinkling bright. And still, it was as though the Bishop-Fish had only just started to talk, yet a century had passed again.

Ascending above the Earth, Roe could see the glittering coastline she was born upon, then the duller lands of Old Earth beyond. She could still see her form upon the rock-garland bed, even as she rose higher and saw all of Gaia in space like a colourful round gem. It gave Roe such a sense of hope, of possibility, *a giant wishing gem*. In a splitting of cells, Old Earth was fading, a hologram, dividing and splitting off into eons of nothing-ness among a trillion other cells.

A galaxy of glowing sea-stars, below and above and far off dazzled her. Her body was gone, the weighty seal skin had disappeared, it was just the stars, stars, stars which began dancing, hovering just for her. The whole eternal sky-sea moved in a complex pattern of inter-entwining swirls and rounds and loops, moving in such perfect unison, and so effortlessly in precision, then the entire midnight indigo firmament engulfed her in pattern, a perfect system performing an effortless never-ending miracle around her. A complete euphoria.

The Selkie understood; this world, this universe of souls and animals and humans and plants and beasts, the seraphim too, were all attending to her, loving her, serving her endlessly. White Fire, white wings. Dust clouds of planets in rosy-gold and soft glowing amber flecked and shone with crystalline sparks of life toward her.

The love was indescribable, invading everything, every particle. Pure, blazing with joy. Light beings, so radiant, with glowing tails and wings and fins stood in all directions and spoke to her. She felt strong, whole, at home. She watched as immense beings, made of light reached forward, pulling the whole ocean in a swirl of a wrist and another hand reached through vapour-clouds offering prisms and geometries, webs and nets that were sheer and gauzy, supple, and moving in sequence.

At times the Selkie fell again into the black frozen underworld, but found that she could will her mind back to the musical colours and light of the sky and singing, she could return to the place of dancing stars and light beings.

A cycle began, of moving between the below and the above, became faster, and repetitive. Roe suddenly moved briskly as if pushed along with a strange new force in both directions. She saw a beach with black prisms of onyx and the white sands of time. She saw a storm that swept in such knowledge in sounds and tones and sparks, a tidal wave that encompassed the Earth, a surge so strong that it levelled mountains and reformed continents. She was caught in a tumble, pummelled as if in the eye of a ripping wave.

This Labyrinth of dark and light within, had no end and no beginning. She traversed it so many times that her skull ached, and her body hurt. And then a whisper… *just dream my darling just dream.*

A voice finally reached her, and she stirred awake, finding the Mirage women hovering over her, but again she fell under. She lay sideways suspended and her mammalian eyes cross-focused, glazed.

Roe could now not tell what was real and what was not. She awoke fully one day and asked a ream of questions; "Why is there a mask of my face on the wall?"… "Why do you need spares of my face?" and then, "Why do they play this music? Can I ask for something else?" and then she immediately fell deeply back below.

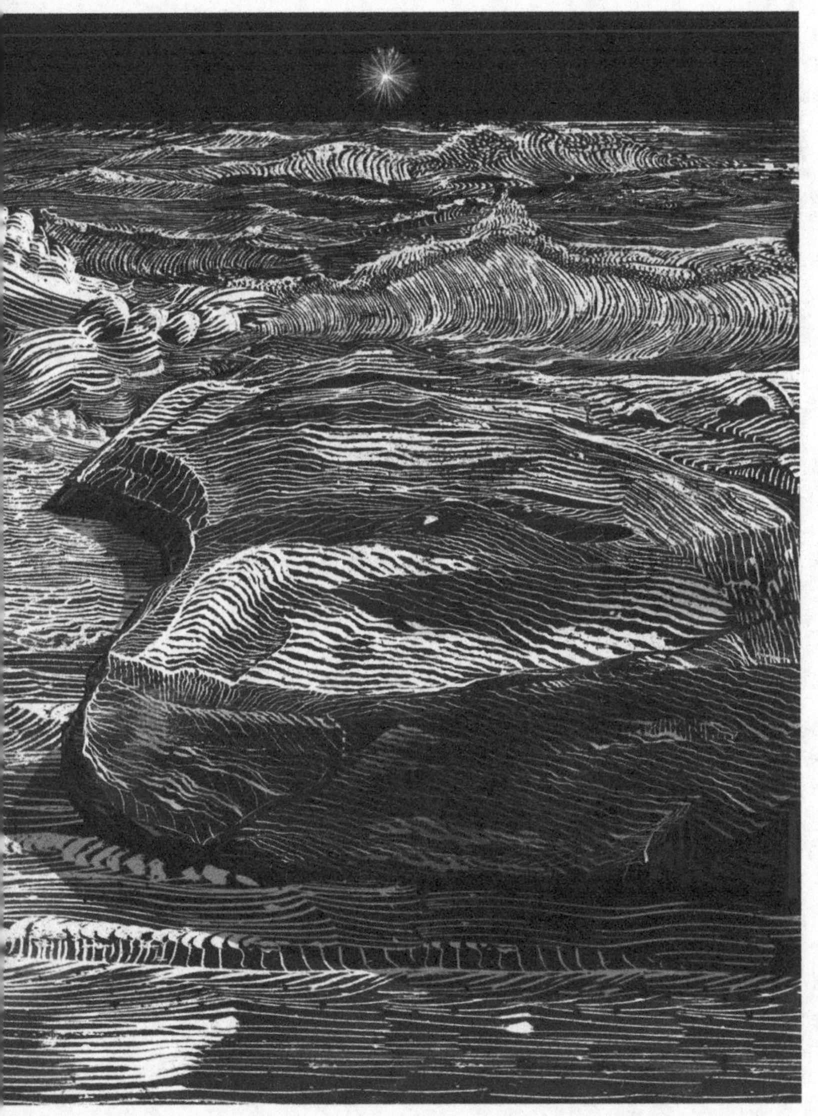

The Bonfire of Self
Orla. ENTRY №:05

Under the glowing alabaster tower, in the sheltered beach nook, I witnessed myself as a marionette guided by strings into the sky. Seeing both from within and without, all clothes were removed. Slowly every layer came off, coat and hood, dress and underskirt, vest, scarf and belt. There was no feeling of cold, just a numbness shrouded in wind chill, an anesthetised shell of skin, exchanged for an improved focus on the interior.

Jewellery and hair was stripped and piled on with the boots and stockings. Collecting driftwood for fuel was a slow shuffling to and fro along the sand, allowing the vulnerability to increase. Toes floated just above the sand.

The figurehead collapsed without breath, a cascade of close-down continued up and down the vertebrae, the face tingled. The aorta, a broken fountain, leaked at the chest. From inside I lost all sight and had trouble sensing parts of my body. In blunt prickles, fear rose, but there were no tears.

Then, liquid intestines, emotional flush, and wild-bruising-dancing began spontaneously, like a lashing on the small beach. I made sense within this whirling plunge into chaos and pain and the puppeteering strings threw me upon the shore in untamed twirls. I scratched and scoured my skin, I shook and swirled and fell.

The watcher with my veneer purged;
wool, silver, mud, ivory, wood, clay… up it
came, lodged deep, it rose up and splattered
on the sand. Things came from even deeper
down, soul triggers, resurfaced, then released
with astonishing noises. I went deeper again
without resistance. The low-keening wince
came on again. A writhing grind over teeth.
An impotent fury unbottled. I shed skin like
a snake, shivering it down, working
backwards, discarding the creation I'd so
carefully and deliberately formed. I think it
was then I died.

Velvet blackness.

In time I rose to sit cross-legged, in the
cold light, tethers cut from a higher hand,
the human spirit had re-entered. I looked to
the skies-day-moon sliding toward the sea.
It seemed to say to me "My influence can
help you, but I don't have the answer".

The only answer is within.

I gripped the notebook, seeing it with
new eyes and hoped to remember the story
when it was gone. I was in a state of ecstatic
surrender as I placed it on the pile of
clothes, hair, skin and driftwood. I sat back
to look upon my un-lit bonfire of self.
Quite satisfied with what I'd built and what I
was prepared to destroy, I struck a match
and set it to the belongings, then kneeling,
watched as the notebook, pictures, the
letters, the stories, and my name, burned.
Flames leapt into the dusk. *Close eyes. See.*

I saw dry green grasses that furiously
danced this way and that. Twigs rattled free
from She-Oaks and splintered across the
bay, airborne and floating. The ocean was
so wide and high it filled the expanse of my
inner vision, a tiered stack of waves that
replaced the sky. Rolling waves seemed so
near, as if I could reach out and touch them,
a veil of white frills and lace billowing

remained, just the cover pages had burned, and the paper leaves rustled in the wind, sandy, damp and smoky.

Leave your words on stone.

I departed the beach, leaving the notebook deep in a natural cloche in the sea cliff. Still captured in a laser clarity I glided toward the tower, viewing the deep pain of needing to be seen and loved on one hand and the need to hide from all sight on the other. I watched the suffering of holding a rope tethered in a tide to the past. *Release the tame habituation, the comfort only suffocates.*

There was a void between old beliefs and new ones that needed to be located and distilled. A process of precipitation and extraction, by slow degrees, that might coalesce into some new form. I set out to reconcile these riddles.

What have I forgotten?

As I reached the level of the Jetty, the Bailiff greeted me with a long mantle of ancient, patched cloth, cloaking it softly around my shoulders. He told me to wait in the tower and swiftly departed. I looked around for the sage smiling guide, but he was also gone.

The Ferry awaited, lanterns lit. I no longer wanted the warmth of the lounge, only to breathe in the cold wind and stay on the Jetty, but the Bailiff was firm.

Spark up in the sun.

Outside the tower I paused for the last ray of pale sunset to charge me. The softest atom of energy could be detected on skin over the cold wind, and I marvelled at the fortunate space of chance between my body and the Sun; its perfect nourishment filling me by osmosis. I could quite clearly see the network of quarks and glimmers that entirely filled the space between the land and the luminous giant of light. I dared not stare into it, knowing its awesome power even at this great distance.

Free now, of old lands, tattoos of places
only behind eyelids, I entered the warm
tower lounge, saw it was closed, so drifted
upstairs to sit in the second storey bay
windows, to rest and examine new seeds of
thought and wait for direction.

CHAPTER SIX
The Exploding Mirror

Many years passed and Roe grew into a young girl with a coppery-orange pelt growing steadily at the back of her neck. A clean sun-bleached cloth was placed upon her skin each day. Yet still she remained, in the eyes of the Mirage, as unconscious, asleep on a garland of rock, her foretold destiny uncertain.

It was agreed that Roe would be raised in the Mirage Sanctuary. A child had never lived here before, as they could not possibly realise or sustain the frequency required, but Roe seemed to resonate with the environment and did not evaporate even in her sub-altern state. She lay in a healing cave at the sea-level of the sanctum, close to warm geysers of underground steam.

The women, both the young Acolytes and most senior Anchorites, took turns keeping vigil beside the sleeping child.

Roe's cave was ringed with tamala limestone, alabaster and ash. Sink holes at high tides, flushed fresh sea spray into the cavern and Sea Rosemary was left on ledges by young Acolytes assigned to the High Priestess of Healing, whose collective pure focus remained on restorative love and care of the physical body.

While sleeping, the Selkie grew into her terrible hands and feet. The deformities lost their distorted vulgarity, and the webbed fingers and toes were only just discernible. The sleeping child appeared stronger and healthier every day and it seemed that some of the pledges dedicated by the Senior Mirage before Roe's birth were coming true.

It came time for the *Keeper-of-the-Keys*, the Adoratrice, to sit with Roe and tend her. The

Mirage population was not large, so she had completed this task on many occasions and resented it more each time. The Adoratrice still inwardly seethed over the favours bestowed upon the child and felt threatened by Roe's natural-born ability to shape-shift into a seal.

The bullion-gold mirror given as a gift by her parents all those years ago, hung in Roe's cave, out of sight of the Adoratrice who despised it. As she stared into it, her darkest shadows were brought forth. She vexed over the vows which had come to pass and even though she had set a curse in place to strip the child of her endowments, she raged in impatience to see Roe's full destruction.

Woozy with herbs to maintain a false frequency, she had tried ever since Roe's birth, to return to her lay and devotional duties in the Senior Mirage, feigning compassion when guiding new Acolytes or wanderers to their caves around the island, smiling falsely as she checked over stores and distributed provisions. But the mirror revealed all her ugliest ambitions and horrid truths she refused to face.

"I should be the one with the grand destiny! I am the most powerful of all the Priestesses! Why this upstart? Why this child? It is *HER* fault I cannot focus on my tasks and devotions! It is *HER* fault I cannot attain peace of mind!" The priestess paced Roe's cave wringing her hands and beseeching her devotions in a treacherous sham. "I have been so long good to you Divine Mother Earth! Divine Father Sun! So long here in your service! It is I who should be so favoured!"

Upon this occasion, after a brief glimpse in the mirror, the Key Keeper suddenly decided it important to remove Roe's pelt growing at her neck and lopped it off without hesitation in one swift slash and threw it deep into a labyrinthine cave.

This act was beyond redemption of the panacea she usually imbibed to stay in constancy, and the Key Keeping Adoratrice fell through the veil, finding herself in dirty littered caves, her anger and bitterness lowering her vibration into dark realms. She had wily ways to make her way back to her position of power and appearance in the Mirage and now with the pelt concealed and Roe's truest gift removed, she schemed further how to evade detection of the full wrath of her wretchedness.

Her gatekeeping had turned to poison, for now the Key Keeper had lost all control, and found herself calling upon the Sea Wolf of the Islet capes to visit that very evening at midnight, under pretence of some vague benefit.

The Adoratrice hoped the Wolf would not be able to resist the plump morsel of flesh lying on the stone altar and would naturally do her the service of removing the Selkie from her sight, absolving her of charge, fault and guilt. At the least, she could blame the Wolf for removing the seal pelt.

The Wolf was very hungry. He was born hungry, his soul thirsty. Nothing quenched it. He arrived at the Sanctuary and was drawn by the Key Keeper into the warm underground grottoes of the island to where Roe lay.

The Wolf entered the flickering room of stone and water. He caught the scent of the Selkie quickly and a distant flicker of craving rose like lightning through him. A *HUNGER* memory. That lit him up so sharp.   An insatiable thirst for blood, soft, flesh, a bite…*a taste*…

Roe had been stirring for days…her inner thoughts were roaming into her body again, bringing her to the surface, she could hear the cave echoing… The Wolf jumped upon the rock bed where the Selkie lay, biting immediately into flesh hard, into the wrist, tasting sweet blood…*and an eerie morning years ago…*

Roe's eyes snapped open upon the Wolf and his gaze sank to hers, then to her other wrist which bore the bite-scar of his own mouth. The Wolfs eyes widened, *It's her! It is…her!*

The Selkie ripped her bitten arm away and sat bolt upright, reaching instinctively for her pelt and felt only a soft head of hair. Roe was AWAKE! The Wolf pulled away, unsettled for hurting her, but certainly not sorry. He stood by now, shackles pierced. The Selkie turned to the Adoratrice and yelped, "Where is my sealskin?! Bring it to me NOW!"

The Adoratrice moved toward Roe and the Wolf, shocked that the child was fully awake and enraged that the Wolf was backing away.

"Well eat her then Wolf! Take her! Feast upon her!"

Instead, the Wolf leapt straight at the Key Keeper. They stumbled and fought viciously, the Wolf in an undeniable blood-rage.

The Key Keeper pulled a dagger from her mantle and stabbed him deep in the trunk while heaving him into a grotto sinkhole. He splashed heavily below causing' the light bouncing off the cavern walls to speed into a rocking dance as the glow worms lit the foaming water.

"What have you done?!" The Selkie screamed, jumping to her webbed feet and scrambling after the injured Wolf. She hit the cold dark seawater and Selkie blood shape-shifted her body. Her mammalian eyes focused and she saw the Wolf sinking, inert, to the sea bottom.

She swam down strongly and grabbed him, he awoke underwater and began to struggle with her, pulling her back down instead of to the surface. She tried to untangle herself from his paws, but his weight clung to her, he climbed her body, pushing her deeper underwater, scratching her with his claws, kicking her arms, her chest, then her face, drawing blood once again.

Without her pelt, her lungs burned and the cold set in quickly, making limbs sluggish. She surfaced behind him squealing and scrambling onto the rock, "You almost drowned me! I was trying to save you!" He swung around to face her, "You almost drowned ME, and I was trying to save YOU!" the Wolf growled, clutching her shoulders, baring down his eyes into hers.

"Nooo! I was trying to save you! I DID save you! You can't swim Wolf!"

"You didn't save me!" the Wolf scoffed, "I saved myself, I could have killed you just now! Eaten you! But I didn't, I protected you instead!"

"Not killing me is your idea of saving me?"

"I saved you the day you were born! I brought you back to life!"

Roe almost laughed in disbelief. The Wolf was so familiar, his incubi spirit had stormed her coma on many occasions. She wanted to embrace him yet here they were, in seething conflict.

"No." Roe shook her head furiously, breathlessly, "When I was born you bit me, and nearly killed me then too! I raised myself back to life!" Roe was exasperated, suddenly cold and weak. She had given all she had to retrieve him from the seabed.

The Wolf continued, "That's twice! Twice I've revived you then! When you were born, I roused your pulse, and just now I saved you from the Adoratrice, she wanted you DEAD."

"You're bleeding Wolf, you need help...I awoke myself, don't tell me what I know...your just..."

They had climbed clear from the water, back into Roe's cave, still arguing, imploring, locked in ravishing anger and sparks, when suddenly the glass face of the golden mirror exploded with such force, so loudly, a *shock-burst* BOOM! of sound echoed across the cavern, producing a silent truce between them as fragments of broken glass hit the stone floor at their feet.

The Key Keeper stood back in amazement, a bloodied knife still in her rigid hands. As the sounds of many feet echoed outside the cavern with Acolytes, Adepts and Anchorites running to find the disturbance, she hid her hands in folds of her garments and the Wolf, badly wounded, slunk away into shadows.

Roe, having finally fully awoke, picked up a shard of mirror-glass to see who she was.

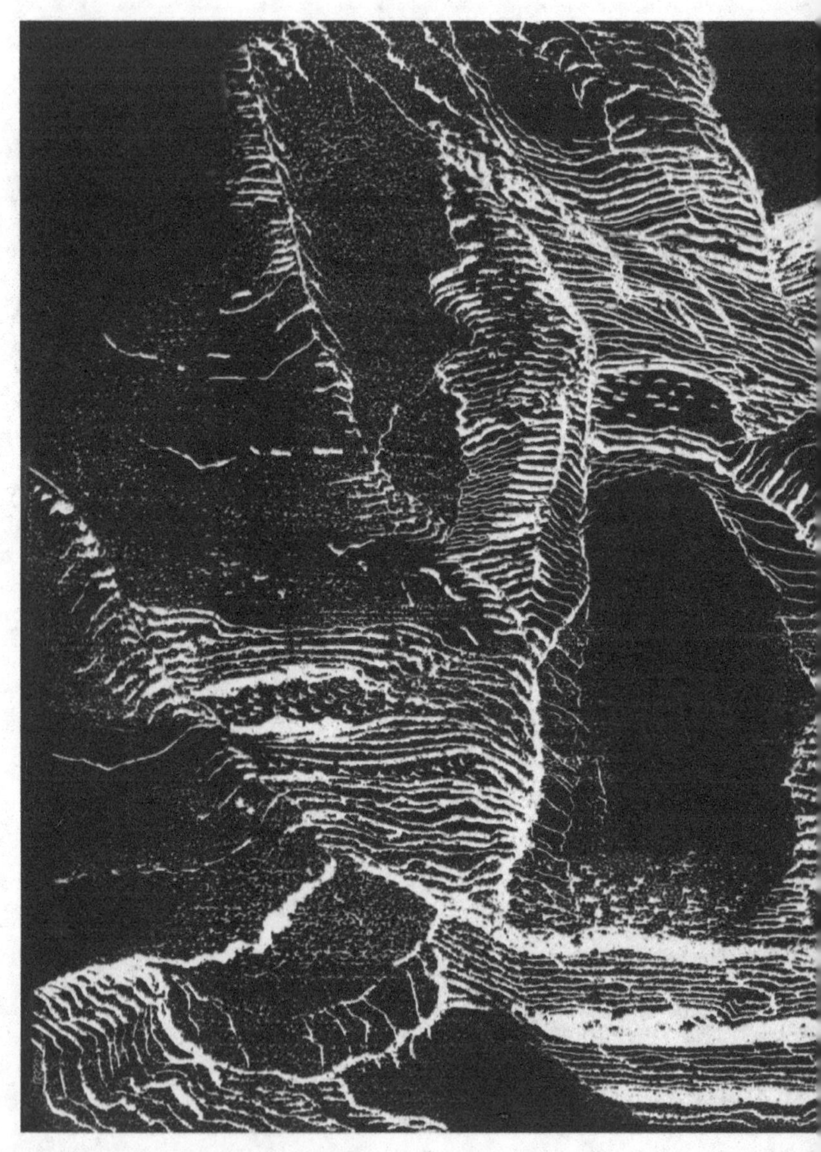

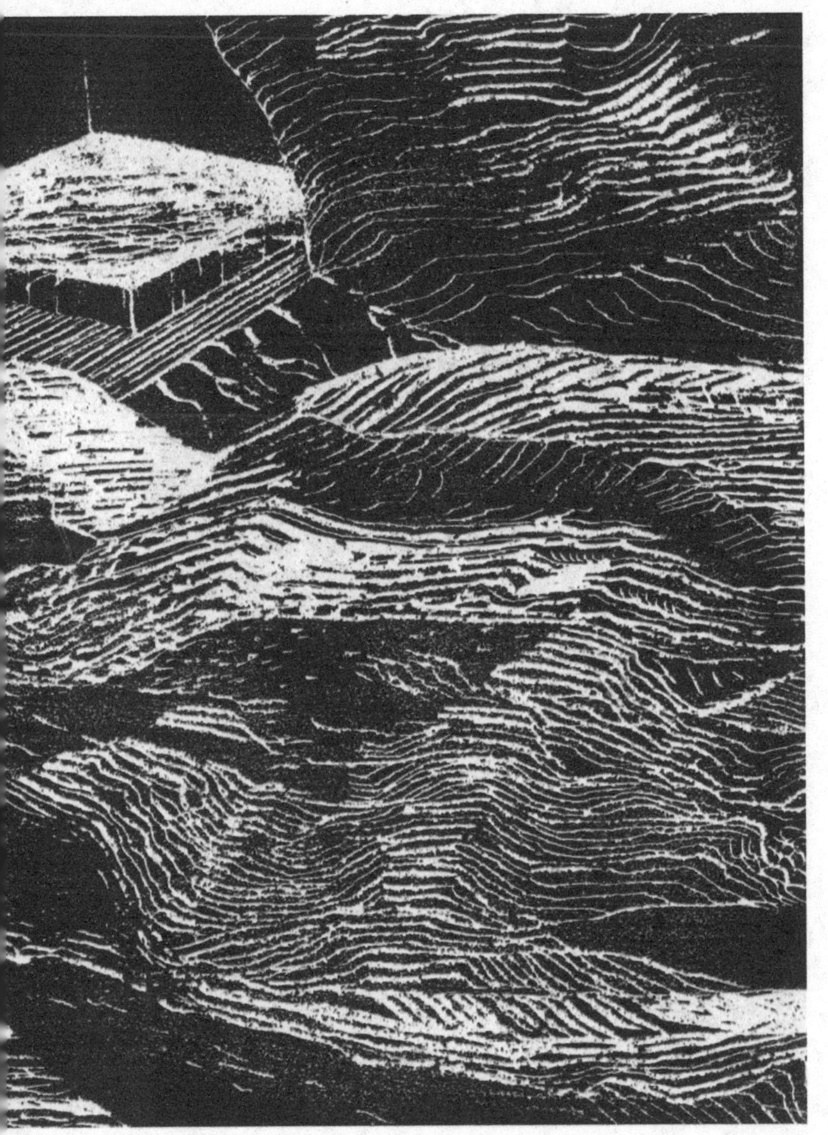

Window of Perpetual Dusk
Orla. ENTRY №:06

From the second tier of the tower, I could see further out to sea. The twilight was perpetual. Time had ceased, or perhaps slowed. All possessions were gone, my mind opaque. The watcher and the marionette had ceased their struggle. The alabaster rooms were magnificently warm, smoothly radiant.

A large round table sat in the bay windows with just one chair. Small windows in the opposite eastern wall would let in shafts of light in the morning I imagined, marking the tilt of the Earth toward the Vernal Equinox.

Would I still be here in the morning?

There was time to ponder the activation at the shore. I felt amidst of some major premonition, or epiphany, of which the feeling was so delicious I almost hoped the riddle would not be solved and I could stay in this state of mystery, relishing in its disturbing power and inscrutability.

I sat with my existential riddle – the heart of Hermeticism realised, the secret of my inner self stripped of pretence to a raw self that I understood as sacredness within. Not a deified humanism, but an integration of divinity well beyond narcissism. A *knowing* of being-ness as a pure spore of the grand whole, made manifest in flesh, revealed through this transcendent state.

I saw the difference between the rite and the ritual. The Rite as the inaccessible revelation and purpose of ritual; to succumb completely to that ineffability as a tangible kingdom to roam.

Is the initiation complete if I feel I have died? *There is no completion. Only continuation.*

It barely mattered. An inner freedom had been grasped, the whole point of the initiation. The void of self, had to be reached. Truly reached, even momentarily, so that the nothingness could paradoxically produce a spring into a real relationship with the divine. The true cry from the heart, answered. An ongoing conversation, commenced in earnest.

Out the window I could see the Barge to the Old World, tethered next to the smaller ferry to the outer Isles. Suddenly panic arose again.

"You've come a long way".

It was the smiling sage. Standing in the doorway. Did he mean my journey here from the other side of the planet? Or the shedding on the beach?

"We recognise your desire. We see your commitment. You are almost ready to sail. What do you think holds you back?"

"Fear. I thought I'd conquered it until I saw the Barge just now." I answered.

"You are outgrowing who you once were, shedding skin like a snake. We know you've shed many. You spiral ever closer to the truth as illusion falls away. You are completely on schedule for what is new." He then peeled with laughter.

"You have acknowledged the past losses which torture you. You greet the shadows and dance with them. You welcome the light that revives you, yet somewhere there is a gap that requires more attention. Know that healing is never an ending point, but an ongoing acceptance to arrive at your wholeness."

He moved closer to me as he spoke, so I could see the depth of the splendid wrinkles on his face.

"The place where the light wants to shine the brightest can be difficult to find, it is the place of the deepest wound, and the greatest transformation. There is no rush. Gather yourself, until it is time to board. Awaken to your actions."

"I understand what you say. My fear is which boat I will board. I fear time is a circle to fall from. I've come so far, but I block my own path with doubt I can't shake. All my metaphysical studies, the Hermetica… the books of the Cumuean Sybil, I brought them …in my notebook… they are left now on the beach…"

"Metaphysics only aims to classify the invisible, intelligent forces, whereas you are in need of experiencing them, not identifying them. Keep listening for the voice behind the awareness. Listen deeply. Fear and doubt cannot exist where you want to go. Another way to see it, is that you cannot exist there if you possess fear and doubt."

The smiling guide was generous and patient. I sensed he was going beyond his usual duties. He calmly continued.

"You have time. You have indicated the importance of analogy, of which can only help you so far. Myth too, will provide a stage, but you should not become deformed by its parameters. Be willing to go where the allusions are the deepest and the barriers are the highest. You may be here for some time, but eventually being will co-incide with knowing."

He paused as if to gauge the depth of understanding, then pointing out the window and down to the beaches, he went on with his guidance.

"The phenomena that appear in your experience – are no accident, they are sent for you only. Use solely the logic of symbols, interpret them in your heart centre, not your mind. Speak now to the wind, allowing your throat to be a chimney of the heart. Uncork your heart. Take your measure, there is no rush. Spend time on these shores, all departures can be delayed."

"Thank you, Sir. Can I ask your name and how long you've worked here?"

"My name is of no consequence, because I am only a mirror of yourself. I am you. You are me. It means you are not alone and never will be." He smiled warmly again. And another peel of hearty laughter. "Remember to let yourself out." He left me to sit and think in the window of perpetual dusk.

CHAPTER SEVEN

Cove of Waterfalls

The Wolf was long gone by the time the remaining senior Mirage had all filed in to the healing cave. Acolytes eavesdropped around in a gallery of excitable whispering. The Adoratrice; *Keeper-of-the Keys* had assumed a benign pose. All seven Senior Mirage High-Priestesses gathered in closely around Roe, urging her to lay once again upon her rampart of rock while she dabbed at the scratch marks lashed by the Wolf.

Compassionate yet intimidating, their long-robed hems were swollen with watery stains of green and blue. Their hair was seaweed and cloth, their hands worn, their eyes and fingertips blue-black with ink. Every inch of the Priestesses' skin was engraved with tiny script-like tattoos; gene-key diagrams, codes and hermetic symbols.

Roe was informed she had been sleeping for fifteen circles around the sun. Fifteen Earth years. She was reminded of the gifts and curses placed upon her; the birth promise, the strength and merit, favour and protection, the strong instincts, but there was no need, she had discerned all that had come to pass. Refusing to lay down any longer, she swung up to stand firmly on webbed toes, speaking in a gush.

"But the Adoratrice declared I would lose these gifts…she wants me dead! She played the Wolf to attack me! And where is my pelt and why was it removed? Please bring it to me at once! And what of my family? My mother, my father? Where are they? And the Bishop-Fish, where is he, I seek his council!"

The Adoratrice's face braced in artificial concern. "We know nothing of the Bishop-Fish. You are confused and still dreaming

Selkie. I would never harm you. The Wolf was the last of your return to the surface, he is your animus, he haunts you, wakes you, antagonises and deludes you. He removed your pelt, his voice is your self-doubt in vile criticisms, do not listen. You are awake now and are ready to face your destiny."

"What is my destiny?"

The Abbattissa, *Ministerial-Mother* answered, "We cannot tell you Roe-Selkie. Only time will tell. You have the Mirage's indulgence; we are here to offer you lessons. The only thing you have of your old world is this, it was clamped in your fist."

The Priestess gave Roe a bleached white bone roughly in the shape of a crescent moon. The Selkie knew somehow it was her grandfather's jawbone, a broken row of white teeth and one gold wisdom tooth still proud in the socket. His big kind dark eyes, broad smile and fish kilt loomed somewhere in memory or dream.

The Abbattissa continued, "Your parents are on the other-side Roe. You are orphaned and belong here now. You will be given new rooms to rest, and you will become an Acolyte, learning the ways of the Mirage. You must choose which High Priestess will be your mentor, do not hesitate in your decision – the first inclination will be correct…"

"Then I choose the Adoratrice, I will follow the Key Keeper and learn her ways".

The Selkie looked squarely into the eyes of the Adoratrice, baiting her guise. Still reeling from her awakening and the swift swathe of events, she didn't know whether it was instincts or madness that had vowed her to this woman.

Roe spent the next fifteen years in the service of the Key Keeper, learning the undertakings with other Acolytes *In-becoming* and despite being well treated, she still did not trust the Adoratrice, who hood-winked her doubts by saying such things as, "no-one else arrived with such ease," and "only pain teaches and so my curse is a gift."

As Acolyte to the Adoratrice she learned the caves, halls and secret passageways of the Mirage Isle. She met with many wanderers that made it over the veil and gave them rooms to rest. Most of these searching souls would quickly disappear, losing faith, but occasionally one would display fortitude enough to join the Sanctuary or the Brotherhood in the centre of the Isle whose tasks in service to the Mirage's cause were also endless.

The Selkie knew which keys opened the library and which opened the infirmary and the teaching sanctuaries. She knew which keys opened the dry-stores and each Priestesses' quarters, even the Sybil's rooms behind the library. She knew how to access the Adyton, the innermost 'holy of holies', the small shrine set deep under the Cardinal Cathedral.

Every action of the Mirage as a whole was in anticipation of the next deluge, the great flood that would come and wash away Old Earth, breaking the last of the mirror-filament threads that kept the Isle in place and releasing it upon a fresh tide.

The Navigator and her entourage of Acolytes, plus many others, worked on the Ark-Coracle every day, which sat nestled tenuously in the knuckles of the mountain ridge above the Sanctuary. It would sail only fifty souls, and it was understood and accepted that not everyone could possibly embark.

Meanwhile, the building, planning and preparing for the cataclysm that was to come moved steadily closer and speculation about whom would sail increased. The Abbattissa would decide on the final crew, twenty-five females and twenty-five males.

The evacuation sequence was practiced regularly, the seed jars maintained, the animals cared for, and provisions updated. All Acolytes knew the signs of the forthcoming flood and took their measurements and observations daily, awaiting the great moment. Everyone had a job to do.

Fifteen more winter-solstices came and went while Roe contently studied her lessons with the other Acolytes, who each told a harrowing story of arrival. It was often implied that Roe had skipped initiation, which set her apart from the other Acolytes. Roe doubled down in her studies, memorised quantum equations and light languages, made her devotions and practiced the dances, fulfilling her duties with purpose and joy from dusk to dawn, then falling into a deep and sound sleep at night.

Eventually Roe began to question her position in the Mirage and started to secretly search for her pelt, which she sensed every day, but could not find. The Selkie had been told her whole life that her destiny would come one day, and her gifts would then be stripped away.

So, one day, without the Adoratrice's approval, Roe visited Sedna's cave, the desiccated old Sybil whose days were surely numbered.

"Please help me, Sedna, it is time I understood your prophecy."

"I am only a vessel Selkie-child. I can merely repeat it for you, as I recall it. Perhaps that will be enough."

"I am ready to hear it afresh Sedna. Please tell me again what you saw in my destiny?"

Sedna picked up her spool and her needle and glazed her withered milky eyes ahead. "You will sail the Ark-Coracle when the waves come. We know what this means. Yes? You are assured a position on the Coracle."

"But why Sedna? Why? What have I to offer? There are many Acolytes more devoted than I, many that are more adept, more dedicated, with more knowledge, I am suddenly riddled with ambivalence, why am I chosen, why do I not just disappear like the other lost and doubtful ones?"

The Sybil continued to weave and thread her needle with her blue-black hands upon soft-dyed jutes and linens. "You will release a vault of flutes with nets of knowledge, the light of which will build an eternal Sanctuary for all. That is what I saw."

"I remember these words Sedna, but they mean nothing to me."

"There is no more to be said Roe-girl. Except this…Your spirit is of the chimera in you, and it does not leave or waiver. Call it back in if it tries to escape. Talk to your new self, and do not be mesmerised by your own narrative. Have faith." And she moved to her weaving loom in the recesses of her bio-lumined cave.

Roe set off that very same day alone, through the shady orchards, through the caves and tunnels, past valleys and beaches, hungry for places she had never roamed. Her destiny seemed difficult and blighted. The missing pelt surely had something to do with her sensation of incompleteness, so she decided it was time to visit the Wolf. If she was to believe the Adoratrice, who had been her mentor for these many years, then the Wolf had removed her pelt and might know where it was. She was wary of the Wolf, but curiosity and yearning had dissolved her fear.

Roe spied the Wolf pacing the high cliffs, and approached him quietly, suddenly appearing before him. A deep knowing disclosed that he would not devour her, even if it was his strongest desire. With instant recognition, the Wolf greeted the black-eyed Selkie with eyes twinkling.

She saw his scars and wounds and understood them. She sensed still the savagery of his uncontrolled impulses and the effort it took him to remain poised. They sat together and looked out to sea. The Wolf told the Selkie about the eclipse of moths that lived in his cave, and she told him about the galaxy of sea-stars that lived in hers. They talked for many hours, then finally Roe pressed in with her challenge.

"Wolf, why did you remove my pelt and where is it now? Please tell me you buried it somewhere, perhaps as a memento of me?"

The Wolf did not like the Selkie's inference of their unspoken bond, even though it seemed a certain truth. It threatened his libertine, and he became dreadfully angry.

"Why would I keep a memento of you? You are no such special thing. Just a vain and pathetic girl who has lost her seal pelt. I know nothing of it. You assume too much. Ask the Adoratrice, I told you the truth when I said she fears your power when you wear it. I would sooner eat you alive than keep your skin hidden somewhere."

Shocked and hurt, spirited notions crushed, Roe wished to run, but quickly asked about her parents. She could see that things were turning sour, that it was time to leave.

"Your parents are back in the expiring old world Selkie. But you cannot go there because you believe too fiercely. You were born here when you died at birth. You cannot imagine there is another place other than this. And on the other side, they cannot believe that this place exists. But I've been there and back again many times." The Wolf was cold and cavalier and would no longer meet her gaze.

"How is it that you can come and go then Wolf?"

"Because I trick myself."

"Well then, why can't I do the same? I want to see where I am from, I want to talk with my parents and understand why I was forsaken."

"We are all abandoned Selkie-girl, don't be such easy prey." The Wolf saw Roe's need to flee and her desire to bridge the threshold but thought her sentimentality a weakness. Never-the-less, he said, "I'll show you. I'll take you to where I cross over, and I will trick you. But first... We play!"

Roe followed the mercurial Wolf to the quiet lee side of the island, where disintegrating tessellations of basalt rock were strewn about in alive shapes and the forest was densely winged and startling.

The Wolf lit a fire on the beach for frolicking under a quivering pitch of sky. They laughed and sang and leapt from rock to rock, blushing, combing and tumbling. The owls joined in their revelry from the tops of trees, hooting and screeching and the crickets were louder than ever remembered. Fireflies zapped around the fire in a frenzy and the ocean crashed in chorus. Shooting stars burned bright and quick in perfect searing flashes.

Early the next morning the Wolf led Roe to a sheltered cove hidden in twists and bends of the Islet, which came into view as they descended through the oldest part of a dark forest. A broad waterfall gouged out of the cliff behind the cove and the pair scrambled down steep hummocks of sand and fern and stone to its crashing feet, where a small clear green lagoon lapped around white sand. The Wolf gave her a plant to chew, then said;

"Swallow the leaves. Behind that waterfall is an old Temple. If you go through and see it, you have crossed. If you swim through the waterfall and it is not there, then perhaps you cannot go through."

"So that is the trick?"

"In part. The trick is you need to find someone you know well from the other-side and speak to them in your mind. It will create an opening that will let you slip through."

"But I don't know anyone on the other side, I never met my mother or father. My grandfather is dead, but he did visit and sing to me many times while I slept, and I have this?" Roe held up the crescent jawbone and gold tooth she wore as a necklace.

"It might work Selkie. Go down to the spot where the water creates a curtain and see if you can locate his spirit. When you hear his voice or sense his arm on your shoulder, enter the waterfall. If you see the Temple, you can go in and inquire after your parents."

The Selkie did as the Wolf instructed. Waist deep in the lagoon facing the torrential waterfall, she turned back to the Wolf, her unlikely and nebulous friend.

"How will I come back again?"

"Remember our beach and listen for my voice, I'll hear you."

"Can't you come with me Wolf?"

"No. I walk alone. As do you. But I'll hear your voice to return. Self-fulfillment is a solitary quest."

With the Wolf's cold reassurance that she could return, the Selkie closed her eyes and shimmered her senses with her grandfathers' face, his giant Seal eyes, his laughing violin…his booming voice…..*the gold tooth in the mandible*…

Roe dove under the crashing-bright waterfall and emerged beyond it into the pit of its shadow. She saw a faint light, and stark towering fissures of grey stone steps leading up out of dark choppy ripples.

The Wolf departed the cove, passing the Adoratrice on the ascending path, who smirked and nodded under her hood of rags.

Lantern in the Forest
Orla. ENTRY №:07

The delayed departure seemed a generous gesture. An allowance to grasp the unfolding. Or was it a test? To see if the veneer's voice-of-fear would begin rationalising and taking control again?

The physical structure of self was dissolving, mental structures disintegrating. All certainties had evaporated. So was any idea of what was to come, which became the central truth I dwelled upon; *All is Illusion, past and future. There is only now.*

I resolved to see more of this place of impasse and so returned outdoors to the windy low-light of the mid-winter eve. Outside the alabaster tower, lanterns had been lined up on the stair by invisible staff and I took one to light my path. I would tread through this process, with the watery sun constant, white, pale and unmoving over the sea, and the moon bright, in-half and winking above it.

Speak now to the wind, allow your throat to be a chimney of the heart.

I planned on walking long enough to draw out the verge of the epiphany, tipping its face toward me. I sensed the core of it, understood it holistically, but needed to step inside-under. The jump from knowing to being, akin to throwing the stone in the lake, and then becoming the ripple.

Speaking at first quietly within, walking fast to keep warm, I entered into the well-worn trails of the tunnel-like grassy floored forest of willowy peppermints, the shushing sea to the left. Pulling over the hood of the

long mantle given to me by the Bailiff, I
understood now its purpose of withdrawal
and disguise.

I walked for countless hours, listening for
a true inner voice and delighting in the
conversations when I harkened the soul,
registering and recording its parameters, the
tone and cadence, its difference in quality to
the false-voice of veneer's jibes of wreckage
and threat.

The wind was loud enough to warp any
words released by the throat, obliging a
quick weighing of their strength and truth as
they emitted. I requested the whole body
listen to the phrases streaming from the
mouth, every thread, line and sentence
became counted by the energy centres along
the vertebral column of bones.

Under the self-moving hood of isolation,
I noticed at the periphery a change in
colours upon the landscape. A blood-red
orb in vermillion cloud, imperial and distant,

now met the vanishing point on the indigo-sea. The sun appeared through intervals of brambles and coppice, branches and twigs silhouetted black and thousand-fold in a graphic tapestry against the blazing pitch of sky.

Hundreds of seabirds spiralled up, petrels, shearwaters and albatross, billowing on breezes and arching on beams. Rabbits and kiwi's, sat in open mossy grasses, orange light reflected in their eyes, frozen and staring into it. Emus and moa birds chewed under the Moonah trees, hypnotised too, by its overpowering glory.

Pausing at an open break in the giant Peppermint trees, I set down the lantern so palms and temples could absorb the sunset. All of a sudden, I noticed a gigantic owl, camouflaged within the tree just metres from my face, startling me such that a hot static rose and spread over me like a rash.

The owl faced inland, away from the sun, tucked into shade completely still. It blinked and hooted, then nodded the way I'd come, then became utterly still again, a silky statue.

Quite clearly, this was a moment that required little deciphering.

This is the point of return.

CHAPTER EIGHT
The Arid Temple

Roe swam forward from the waterfall, onto steps. A small Temple of rock stood entombed in the cliff face, its windows blinking eyes. For the hundredth time, she yearned for her pelt and its layers of super-natural protection.

The air was heavy, muffled, a smog of sickly grease. Crumpled papers and piles of ugly refuse lay about. Bleached shells without shadow or weight sat grimly around dusty altars of crumbled rock. Roots and weeds and rotting sea litter piled up in every corner. Sitting forlornly on a stone bench inside the apse of the Temple was a single priest, dirty, tired and emaciated.

"Please Sir, I am looking for a Selkie woman and a Fisherman that lived in these parts thirty years ago. Can you help me?"

"Girl, there is not much left now. Very few people. They are blind with despair, wandering lost, their spirits long departed. Earth has all but died. It is choked. I am lonely here, who would return from the Isle? Why ever would you want to leave?"

"I want to find my parents and bring them to the Sanctuary. I never met them. They don't know I'm alive."

"Go to the old wharves. I heard of a Fisherman who was forbade to leave there by the Mirage. Perhaps an old wanderer will remember him."

Departing the Temple, the waterfall had vanished and instead a dried-up creek bed trickled, stained brown and purple, snaking grime into a burnt and treeless coast. Smoke billowed out black on the horizon and the air smelled acrid. The beach could not be seen, instead a trillion plastic flotsams murked upon the tideline, an ossuary island of effluent ugly shapes.

A rusting wharf, reached out into an oily sea. The sky was dank yellow. The sun burned hot through smoky clouds. All colours blurred without contrast. No fish leapt in the shallows and no birds circled overhead. The only birds were burned and grounded, their feathers tarred and beaks misshapen. Tangled metal in hostile bundles lay about. Roe now understood the anxiety and discomfort of the Old World. At the wharf, a solitary Fisherman, recognised his daughter immediately.

"My child! You are the spit of your mother! Oh, my child, we have thought of you every-day all these years!" The two embraced at length and the Fisherman led Roe to a sideways den of rusting tin, clinging to the wharfs edge.

Roe's mother Lyra sat in a window over the water. She was small and ashen limbed, her hair reddish-grey over giant black eyes with dark freckles across her nose. Lyra's mind melted into her heart when she saw Roe. They held each other and Lyra explained that when Roe died at birth the grief had sent her mad. Lyra led Roe to a hole in the wall. The Fisherman watched on, scalding with emotion, remembering lost seeds, forgotten paths and brimming catches of days gone.

"This is why you've come. I see the scar at your neck. You will need this." Lyra handed Roe her own sealskin, soft 'and musky handled.

"No, Mother! Father! I have my own! I've only lost it, I'll find it again, I came here to take you back; to take you back with me to the Isle…It's so beautiful there, I didn't come to take anything from you!"

"We have waited for you to come for a long time. The Bishop-Fish came to tell us you would arrive like this one day and we have lived for this moment. We cannot leave here, we have tried, again and again to come to the Isle. I am happy to give it you my daughter, it is for your destiny!"

"But this means you will never see your own family under the sea again Mother. It is too much to take from you."

"I give it freely to you, my daughter. Why should I have a pelt, if you don't have one? Besides, our under-sea family have mostly perished. Newborns are deformed and cruelly ill, the water is too warm and full of toxins, the seabeds are dead. Take the pelt and go back to the Mirage, take our stories of the Old World with you, they are stored in the pelt – just listen when you wear it."

"Where is the Bishop-Fish? Father? Why can he not help us now? Come with me, please!"

Her Father answered. "We have not seen the Bishop-Fish for ten winters. The Isle is a mystery we do not understand, but you belong there. I will take care of your mother. Go, and know that you are both Selkie and human, you have my smile, my Roe."

She said goodbye to her parents, leaving them with grandfather Selkie's gold tooth. Roe hurried back to the Temple in the rock, suddenly feeling the urgency to return and accept her role in the Mirage.

She called out for the Wolf in her mind from the carbolic waters in front of the Temple, she dwelled in his snarl, his fur, his paws, but there was no waterfall, no change in atmosphere. She went to plead with the forlorn Priest for help, but he had died, his skull already dusty in the heat.

She dove into the brackish lagoon and squealed to her Mirage family, to the Adoratrice even, to anyone who might hear her, she called out for her mother and father and grandfather. But still she remained.

Roe discovered that not only was she trapped on Old Earth but ensnared too, within the rotting Temple asylum. It became a repeating maze of black water and slimy stone that she could not broach. Days, weeks, then whole lunar seasons passed, and every day Roe tried in vain to return.

She searched for the plant the Wolf had fed her and beseeched him to hear her voice, she yelped to the sky, she tried her mothers' pelt, searching the oily lagoon floor, but still she woke in a grave of whales, dead fish and dull senses. Her usual quick mind was foggy, everything became a haze of survival and nights were sleepless, dreamless and suffocating. Her only solace was the cool face of the moon, which she implored every night to return her to the Mirage Isle, vowing never to question or try to leave it again.

Roe retraced her life, her coma in and out of the deepest underworld, her training, and her accumulated moments of fleeting joy.

She realised that the Adoratrice's curse had come true, she had indeed lost everything; her health, strength and merit, her keen instincts and wisdom, the favour of the Mirage and the nightly sleep of peace which she had taken so deeply for granted.

She wallowed in the unworthiness of the Adoratrice's judgement and churned in a sense of pathetic spoilt vanity, and over-estimation of her abilities, just as the Wolf had said. It appeared as if her special fate was to languish in a locked hot noon of numberless moans and salty starvation, eating insects and slugs and befriending horned lizards, crying sorrowfully as she bit off their heads.

Years and years passed and still every day, Roe would call out to her friends on the Isle, but not one soul did she see. Most of all she called out to the Wolf and wondered if he thought of her too.

Dark Night of Veneer
Orla. ENTRY №:08

Despite the cold, and the silent owl looking on from its perch, I uncaged my torso, dropping the mantle, connecting to this incline high on the wheel of the world. Naked skin blazed orange in the flooded mesosphere. For a few mysterious moments the evening star, moon and sun existed in the human eye, with the nightbird as testimony.

The voyage begins at the end of the wound.

Turning my back to the sun, I bowed to the owl and slowly re-robed in the salt-sheet mantle, speaking to the wind of my eagerness to return. The resolve added pressure so that I hurried and the lantern in

my clutch jangled. I spoke to the shuffling
chest.

"My heart, my heart! You are green!
Green like vines and moss and leaves. You
are so whole within this strangers' skin.
Heart, you have looked so far outside, now
look that far within! You've looked out years
ahead, left and right in judgement of
yourself, you have hungered outside for
sustenance and affinity – did you find it out
there in that awful world? Ohhhh! What do
you love heart of mine? Passion, poetry,
beauty, fierceness! Universal truths… Places
where you think God might be… places
such as this!" The wind whipped away the
words and I smiled exhilarated and kept
conversing…

"Places of harmony… where soul work is
taught instead of paradigms of work,
consume, die! Where beauty prevails.
Where songs are sung! Where the higher

purpose is celebrated… where the Mysteries
are honoured!"

I ran, quicker, a tentative spate on bare
feet. The sunset had activated a code of
recall, downloading whole, through the
crown, an image of the realms before-birth,
the place I belonged. It was simply a
recovering of what was always known only
long forgotten. Although breathless, I
picked up the pace even further and kept up
the monologue, the heart unleashing a chute
to the belly; a fiery anger for survival…the
red of the sun…

"Resurgence of those bright souls that
have known the universal truths has been
marginalised, hidden, exorcised, again and
again! The last of the old paradigms must
crumble….old conditionings must be
slashed, exhausted, worn out, worn down,
never to take root or seed again. Old Earth
must be levelled. Destroyed!"

I stopped in my tracks. Irate that these weeds of anxiety could poke through so easily. Allowing them to grow only kept the passage to the Mirage out of reach. Attracting fear through fear. "How do I escape this damn dread that ties me to this place!" I screamed into the wind. "Sweep me away!"

Shadows will always hover, pick over only what you need for action.

My mind would not rest, and I'd lost the heart rhythm, which seemed to circle and beat upon my insides, but not escape. I could not hear clearly. I ran on through the thickets and cliffs, stumbling on the roots of trees, my toes blue chill…I ran into a fearful void as dark descended, the Earth finally turning to close the day, after hovering still on my behalf it seemed, for so long.

Dry thunder rippled a million murmurs toward me, thick cloud gathered, but no rain fell, and no stars, orb or moon could be seen. The sound of the ocean muffled, smothered under wind rustled trees, the direction of the sea became unsure. I was certainly lost as nothing seemed familiar.

I kept moving to keep warm or surely this flimsy form would freeze and die. Existential questions of transfiguration no longer mattered when my very physical survival seemed at stake. Images of black striped devils picking over my bones, sprouted in my mind. Singing to uncork the heart, only dull noises of broken plectrums rasped out gutless. Mutterings exasperated, desperate, whining. Hours passed in dread fear and mumbling panic.

Slowing insane then jubilant, in circles, listening to locate the true voice of the heart, I was tricked by the veneer-voice over and over again. Nothing made sense and all the guides that had brought me this far with signs and visions and messages, now seemed to desert me. My fear now was that this night, the longest of the year, would never end.

The lantern eventually sputtered and died and an angry self, huddled under a tree, a mess of flaying arms… foolish limbs….imagined affinities… lost, lost, lost and so cold, cold cold, in despair. I was out of the body again, watching this incensed animal, wild in her white robe, blue lips and hair flying.

Something split then, the sound of a limb struck from a tree, cracked in two by lightning. It took time to realise the almighty CRACK came from within, I could smell the smoke and burning hair.

You have transformed, spilling from your skin anew. You have been lit. You will make it through this night, you know this, just as you know without doubt, you will see the dawn and you will sail on. Examine your heart and you know this truth. The light of your spirit is a magnificent diamond that will warm and sustain you.

Under that tree of impasse, this radiant voice spoke to me all that long dark windy night and the cold-cracked cheeks of the ego-mask sat aside grieving, knowing it had been downcast, set aside and relegated from the forecharge of this spirit.

Unseated, forced out… the expansion could no longer be erased or rolled back in, the vying for control was over. Light streamed from my every pore, startling the insects who buzzed around my shining head. I had become the lantern.

CHAPTER NINE
Snakes and Ladders

After fifteen years of despondent suffering alone in the dry Temple, Roe awoke one day startled by an entire pillar of rock crumbling to the ground in an almighty crash of dust. It revealed a small niche enclosure where an old book had been hidden and forgotten.

It was a very thick old notebook, surely once belonging to an Acolyte. It contained diary entries, letters, notes, lessons, diagrams and pictures, all of which were utterly fascinating to Roe. Although partially burnt, obscuring dates or an author's name, it remarkably included translations of Hermetic texts and Vedic manuscripts, some of the oldest and most revered documents of humankind. Articles that the Mirage Priestesses had sought after for thousands of years, sat casually in this small folio, with many other unrecognised texts Roe was thrilled to discover.

Roe read the pages thirstily, drinking in the lost knowledge hungrily as if manna, not moving once from her position in the rubble of the wall until she noticed most of the day had passed.

It was not the lost manuscripts, but a diary entry in the notebook, that set Roe's heart beating even faster. Something so personal, in the looping scrawl of this unknown person, shot deep and clear, filling her with the sudden knowledge she would be soon leaving. She had squandered fifteen years there, listening to artificial voices in her head.

Using her mother's pelt like a pouch, Roe placed the notebook inside, waved riddance to the dusty gloom of the arid Temple and waded into the sludgy water holding the words in her mind.

"A curse is simply fear projected at you. Have no fear and the curse has no power. Go within and examine the fear – what is it? See that that the fear, which is only your imagined belief and not a certainty, is the thing that holds you captive. Imagine what your life would look like without any fear and doubt and walk as such into your new day. Listen to the heart, which will speak the truth, then imagine you are a bird and feel how free it is…"

Roe realised her fear was in the false belief of her unworthiness based in the Adoratrice's estimation, or that she was not valued or seen clearly and never would be, by the Wolf, by her parents or by anyone, but her spirits' voice knew the real truth, that she was loved endlessly.

She thought clearly now too upon the words of the old Sybil Sedna. *"Talk to your new self…don't be mesmerised by your own narrative…."*

Roe closed her eyes, clutching her belongings, knowing it was time to release old convictions and return at once to her free spirit. She envisioned the Mirage Isle and felt it tangibly under her fingertips, she saw her future self, smiling, laughing, rejoicing, dancing and swimming in a snug copper-satin pelt and at that moment she asked her future self – "Will you help me?" and future Roe replied, "Of course! Dive NOW!".

A fresh waterfall cascaded over Roe in a thousand blessings. She dared not open her eyes, yet knew without doubt that she had crossed to the Mirage Isle. As the waterfall rinsed years of dust and despair, Roe vowed never to allow anything to dampen her spirit or misguide her inner compass ever again.

Filled with the vigour of new-self, Roe scrambled out of the water, a deep sense of certainty engulfing her senses. The Earth tremored oddly under her toes as she scurried up out of the waterfall cove, up hillsides and across the blessed Isle, the sun emerald, the water indigo, silhouettes crisp, the light hazy glimmers. At the Sanctuary Roe charged through the mouth of the Adoratrice's cave, capturing the Key Keeper stunned and in utter shock at her return.

"Where did you get that Pelt!? You've trespassed my rooms!?" The Adoratrices' head swung about wildly. Why are you here? You don't belong here!"

"This is my Mothers Pelt. So, you did remove it! Say now where it is! Tell me NOW!"

The Adoratrice turned swiftly away from Roe, panicked, culpable and exposed, edging toward her drug bowl, which had been empty since Roe's absence. Flustered, she took a deep breath and tried to maintain a calmness, lest her vibration send her back across the veil.

"It was removed for your own benefit Roe." The Adoratrice turned, smiled stickily, trying to appear unrattled.

"You lie! You fear it, you fear my power, which is only my natural born right. You are riddled with shadow; it is YOU who does not belong here Key Keeper. I will replace your position as Adoratrice. Leave now and do not come back!"

"Ha! You think you can replace me?! You will never outgrow your true self! You are monstrous! Wild! Loh! YOU cannot stay here, you are deformed! You are self-centred! You think you have something to offer the world?! You do NOT! You are without grace! Without esteem, without vision! You bark like a dog and hiss like a snake! A pock-faced troll with two faces that don't belong together! You are pitiful, weak and worthless! You….are cursed, you are…"

The Key Keeper realised that the curse held no more power, none at all, it had run its course. Her full malice and bitterness blistered into terrible features, finally revealed after years of suppression, her limbs and lips began to tremble, and the colour drained from her face.

The six other High Priestesses of the Mirage filed into the sea cave.

"Enough Key Keeper" said the Abbattissa. "You have lost your way. The Isle is a place of alignment with the divine within you, clearly you have forgotten this. You have confirmed our worst fears, and we must ask you now to leave."

The Adoratrice understood then she was banished from the Mirage, she was already dissipating, hovering on the edge of the two worlds, beginning to dissolve, back to Old Earth and the misery there.

"If you are truly holy, you will forgive me! You will not exile me from here!"

"Key Keeper you have proven your heart distorted. The holy forgives yes, but we are guides. We walk among shadows with light, which is love, including self-love and you are harming, yourself and others. You will no longer hold the keys, nor hold the title of Adoratrice.

The Adoratrice attempted to intercede, but Abbattissa's voice boomed louder.

"You must realise that you no longer qualify even as Acolyte. Your drug bowl cannot help you now and your vibration will not hold. A barrier must be raised to your venom, which only spreads and sickens what it comes into contact with. You have raised this barrier yourself. It is time to go back down the ladder you arrived on, or the snake is quicker if you prefer?"

"You cannot discard me! I WILL be heard! You cannot banish me!"

Two snakes slithered along the floor and stopped next to a recess that opened in the floor, where a ladder descended into pure rock beside the caves' sink hole.

The Adoratrice now cooly understood the choice. She walked toward the snakes and ladder, stooping to allow the serpents to climb her body, criss-crossing her frame in their dance of life and death, then in unison, bit her on each side of the neck and receded back to the sand cave floor.

The Key Keeper turned to stone, her limbs cracked and fell, she tumbled into the sink hole, passing through the mirror-threads of space into the abyss. Descending to where she would never be heard, sunk deep, ledged in shadow, arms, legs and fingers scattering, overgrown and vanished from sight, she would dissolve under the palled cloak of Old Earth.

Roe turned to the Mirage and was embraced by all six High Priestesses, in a new circle of potential.

A special night viewing of the sea caves was given as a concert that very evening that lasted until dawn. The entire Island attended, and a new zealousness filled the grottoes. Roe had returned and the all-too powerful Adoratrice and her sagging energy had been banished.

Many sensed that night, that the silken mirror threads that tied the Mirage Isle with Old Earth were stretched tighter than ever before, that a splitting was occurring. The ovum of New Earth was ready to separate the membranes that hosted the twin planets of dark and light.

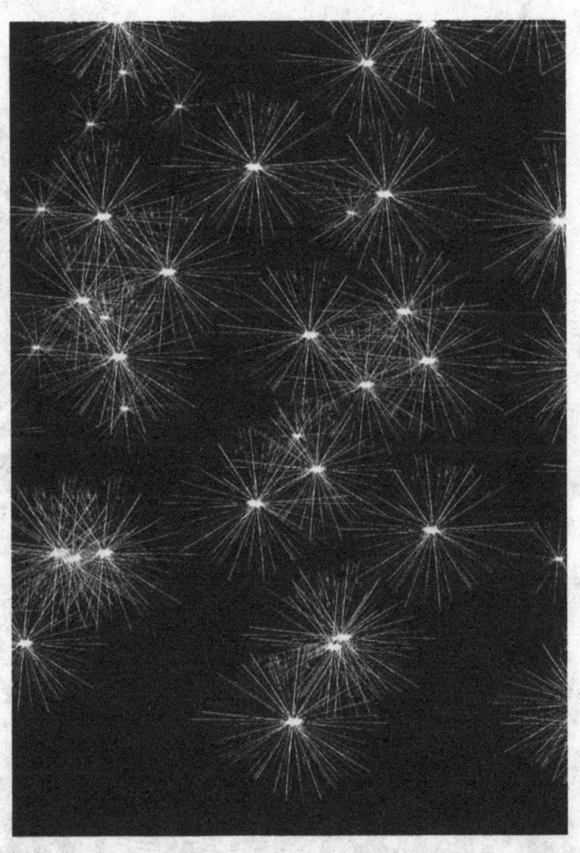

The Glowing tree of Impasse
Orla. ENTRY №:09

By dawn, from the central eye, I felt elevated, floating above the seat of tree roots, all vacillations gone. A glowing rhizome descended from my core, grounding me with encounters of rich, breeding soil. A burning torch struck right through me, from the centre out, with such ignition and sustenance, it overflowed.

I could see peace and connection as a thing, sequenced and gliding as if on a soft river of my highest self. There was no struggle, no barriers, no jagged edges.

The light flooded, gushing from me as a waterfall, the droplets, splashing, dancing, ….transparent…

Become transparent as if jumping light.

I began to laugh. The heartiness turned to a raucous hilarity and full dispensation of any possible remaining dim under the tree and the ones beside. Light bounced down my clavicles and ribs and lit up every facet, radiating out, and through, making me spectral, unseen… the hysteria of laughing swamped me, tripped me, leaving me breathless and tinkling.

A soft crystal with a thousand faces.

The mundane was suddenly radiant and significant, the simple shadow of a tree was a revelation in its shaping as if an Angel.

Eventually worldly sensations returned such as hunger and cold, reminding me that the veneer of self would always have its place, in keeping this body alive, steering me through this experience.

I savoured then that body of skin and flesh, muscles, tendons, nerves and nails that brought me here. I loved that body, the mask, for all its pain, for carrying me this far. I stood and twirled, I sang a giddy song, an expansive non-sensical ridiculous yodel to the dawn sky, which spun all the energy centres faster and faster… I danced, jumping and skipping, delighting in this reversal of command and hierarchy of matter.

The delusion of duality was quashed as I saw the mechanisms in function. A dauntless unification sparked on and on an aliveness and arrival to a place that can never be arrived at, only perpetually realised again and again. The harmony of being in the moment of *now* carried on without vigilance, without a past or future.

The Deep Green Sea
Orla. ENTRY №:10

The rising sun was dilute and low on the horizon as I returned along the coastal path. Light still beamed from my eyes. Behind the tower I retrieved my half-burnt notebook from the little back beach to make this final entry. I can see the Ferryman and Bailiff waiting patiently for me at the Jetty. I know now that the ferry to the Isle is only symbolic. I've already arrived and need only take this last passage to close the initiation which began at the prow of the barge. I think I can already see the women, through the trees, washing their robes and singing.

I must record the vision given by the guide with the shining teeth…

….. The ocean was so wide and high it filled the expanse of my inner vision, a tiered stack of waves that replaced the sky. Rolling waves seemed so near, as if I could reach out and touch them, a veil of white frills and lace billowing toward me. Rapid patterns and wave forms broke over again thunderously magnified…..

…..I can slip now again, so easily over into a state of seeing and the vision goes on…

….. the horizon eventually calms, and there is a simple and serene expanse before me of deep green sea….I stand on a cliff surrounded by others….men, women, babies, children…the Earth was new and fresh…

I will place now this notebook back in the cloche of rock and board the ferry. From the top storey of the Tower, I see the kind sage waving and hear his peals of laughter.

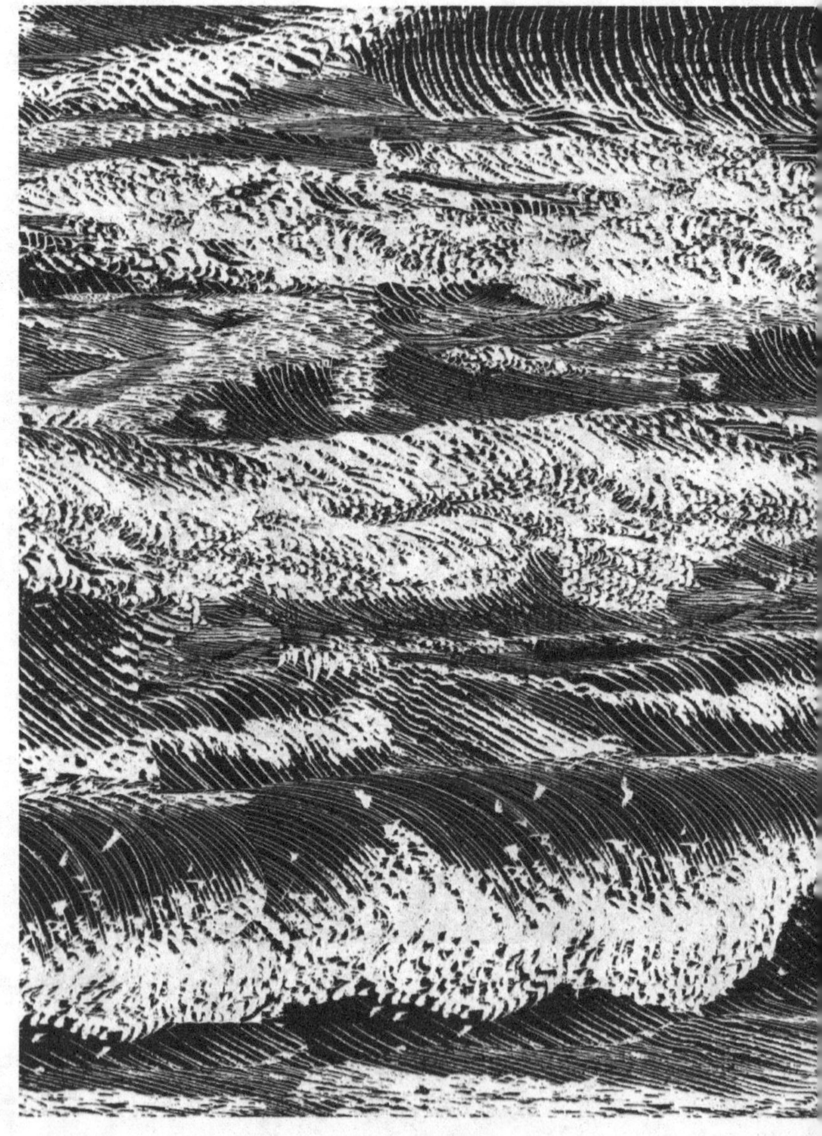

CHAPTER TEN

Sailors Hymn

Deep in the warren of the Mirage Sanctum, Roe awoke late in her own sea cave. She had dreamt of the Wolf in a dark and dreary forest, where she confronted him for leading her across the threshold without a way to return. Roe wanted a reason, an explanation, her hope was that he had not done it deliberately, but he offered neither remorse nor care, forsaking her again. The sighing seaweeds of the Mirage pools and the slap and surge of the fresh sea on the wide grotto shelf, calmed the unease of the dream. She was home. All-seeing shell eyes along the sea-ledge blinked at her in welcome.

Someone had mended the broken glass in the gold bullion mirror. Roe looked straight into her own eyes inquisitively and saw a sailor without-perspective, but a sailor never-the-less. A flicker of fear was in the corner of the reflection, the Wolf racing past. But a newness inside Roe sighed that this soul contract was sealing, the lessons had been gathered. No more chasing shadows, it was time to shine.

The caves were tremoring. It felt peculiarly warm. Roe felt a new urgency to find her pelt and set off to search the Adoratrice's cave. Free now to rummage the caves' recesses, boxes and cabinets, cases and shelves, Roe searched while reminiscing the many days spent in these quarters while *In-becoming*. A memory jumped into her mind, of standing at the central shrine of rock in the heart of the cave and the smirk of insincerity upon her mentor's face.

Turning now to the shrine, Roe shoved at the slab of rock that formed the altar top. It moved ever so slightly and then Roe knew.

She knew her pelt was within the central altar, kept as some kind of reliquary of power for the Adoratrice, who could not wield or control her own. As the stone slab fell to the floor, a chamber full of vagabond was uncovered. Hundreds of ancient scrolls filled the altar void, bundled in cases, crates and bags. A quick scan of the titles on the seals and spines was astonishing:

...Astronomical Maps of Copernicus, Diamond Sutra of Zen... Tao Te Ching...The Fall of Man...The Upanishads...The Bhagavad Gita...Poetry of Xenophanes...Rumi...Medical Botanicals... Discourses of Epictetus....Models of Cosmology... The Tibetan book of the Dead...The Gnostic Gospels...Voice of Siddhartha...The Holy Epistles... Analects of Confucianism...Quantum Codes...

The Adoratrice had been hiding immeasurable missing knowledge, but to what end? Roe realised that the Adoratrice was perhaps much more contaminated than they could ever have imagined. To what benefit did hiding these lost treasures provide her? Other Mirage library texts had referred to these documents, but none had ever been recovered or found. Yet here they were. Did she think these gifts from the tide would secure her a spot on the Coracle? Now they would never know. Jars of jewels were also there, whole crystal vases overflowing with gems; sapphires, diamonds, emeralds and rubies as big as fruit. More books and manuscripts lay under the scrolls and then....

"My pelt!" Roe's fingers in its soft fur was akin to an explosion of all her senses, a melting lusciousness. Its suede interior pliant and flexible smelt like a twin she had known from the womb. Curiously the pelt had grown in tandem with her and after thirty years separated from her body, the seal skin fit sleek like a glove.

As it slipped over her limbs, her wits rose, eyes dilated, lungs and heart slowed, the rush of knowledge gleaned in her journey to the underworld returned in instant fullness; the *giant wishing gem* and dancing stars from her infantile coma rose clearly in her mind once more. She felt dangerously alive.

The whole cave tremored again and with it an Acolyte appeared at the cave entrance calling Roe out to the beach. A shocking view met her eyes as the tideline had risen much higher than had ever been seen, well above the highest ever neep tide.

In just a few more minutes it rose a further fathom, lapping at the entry to the maze network of caves below ground. This was the first sign of the next deluge and Acolytes and Anchorites were already beginning the evacuation process.

The water would rise up first, a great swelling breath under the dome of heaven, then it would recede quickly out to the horizon, draining as if a giant basin released. The the tide would draw back all its power to level Northern Hemisphere lands, before returning to destroy the South.

The electro-magnetic forces could be felt palpably in the air, everyone's hair stood high on end and the birds and animals spun in circles.

Dozens of Acolytes were moving to higher ground, heading calmly but swiftly from the Sanctuary to perform their final and foremost duty for the Mirage, one they had been preparing for centuries.

The entire contents of the library and fresh stores were being moved to the Ark-Coracle. The tidal wave pre-swell was now pouring into the mouth of the Sanctuary caves. In minutes all the living quarters and the Cathedral would be underwater.

Men from the brotherhood joined them now, all hands helped to loosen the ropes and unhinge the wedges that held the Coracle in place. Some souls ran toward the cliff tops, disappearing as they ran, in fear they fell through the veil to Old Earth to endure an ignoble death.

High Priestesses were loading their cases, one eye on the horizon and one eye on their submerging home. Just four mirror ropes of filament remained now holding the Ark in place, devoted men stood squarely, their axes ready to strike the thick threads when the rumble of sea reached a fever pitch before them.

A haunting trail of men and women now gathered holding hands at high ground, facing the sea. The line grew longer as tasks for the release of the coracle became complete. These souls awaited the deluge, welcoming the flood that would annihilate them well before they realised they were drowning. They would witness the end of time. There was no escaping the tsunami that was building, only the knowing that if their assignments were well done, that humanity might prevail elsewhere.

The pre-swell of rising water was smothering the Isle, changing the topography into an unrecognisable new form. The entire complex of the Sanctuary was now underwater. The wind whipped up and changed direction and the rumbling of the Earth increased. Scrambling to higher ground, Roe helped old Sedna who turned to clutch her close with frail arms before speaking.

"Stop now, stop here… the wind has changed, the waters will recede now…well out past the horizon before coming back…these are the last moments for Old Earth…It is only minutes now Roe. Go now and enter the Coracle."

Roe braced the old lady, holding her in the wind. "Sedna, I think I understand my destiny now. The Adoratrice hid hundreds of sacred texts, you will marvel at their titles.

With my pelt I can retrieve them, I can swim down into the caves and save them, they can come to New Earth and help us rebuild the Sanctuary". The wind was streaming furiously now as the ocean sucked down exposing miles and miles of the sea floor.

"Go then Roe, but the caves are flooded now, it is very dangerous. You will have to hurry…Go Roe, go quickly! And goodbye."

Roe gaped at Sedna and saw the Wolf as she did, higher up upon the cliff looking out to sea. Challenging forces now pulled her in multiple directions.

"Why goodbye Sedna? You are on the list!"

"I will stay here Roe, I'm too old to sail. I have a promising new Acolyte, I have named her my successor as Sybil, she boards now, her name is Orla. She will do well. Go Roe, your task is at hand."

Roe let go of Sedna, who smiled into the wind, a look of utter ambient joy upon her face, relishing the strong winds gusting into her long grey hair, her shoulders and chest open, her arms raised to the wind. She appeared as if young again.

Quickly diving into the flooded caves of the Sanctuary, Roe's pelt seer-suckered against her flesh, becoming one with her humanness. Transfigured and alert, all bone and sinew drew fresh salt-blood to extremities, slowing the heart, eyelashes and whiskers became antennae.

In all her forty-five years, this was the very first dive in her truly congruent form as a Selkie woman. The fiddle-strings of her grandfather's violin strummed robustly in every pull of her webbed limbs, clear and invigorating. The pelt held ancestral memory and the recall of visitations from her coma, music, words, voices. She felt charged, complete and adventurous as she swam through the flooded Cathedral. Within minutes she had rescued her mother's sealskin and the Acolytes' notebook from her flooded cave and was skittering back through the Sanctuary.

There was no time to marvel at the dreamlike light pouring through the seawater onto the ancient winding stairs and stone carvings made by the brotherhood masons, now a tomb of sunken debris. She swam switch-like, deep into the dark caves, knowing her way as only *Keeper-of-the-Keys* of the doomed domain could possibly know.

In the Adoratrices cavern, floating belongings nudged the rocky ceiling, wreckage had sunk to the floor or was lost to the heaving forces of sea water. Muffled rumbles of Earth shuddered through Roe's body as she desperately tried to see the scrolls. Her new mammalian reflexes were pushed beyond limit now, even with her wild-eyes seeing, the dim bedlam of the submerged cave made it impossible.

All seemed futile, her fate was finally here; the peak moment was calling, and she could not see a thing. In a breathless despair, her lungs burning, Roe sent thoughts out to sea, to the great Earth Mother, to Father Sun, to the manta rays and dolphins that carried her from the coma of the underworld, to the Bishop-Fish and the beings of light and dancing stars of beyond…."Please!…Help me NOW!"

At once the cave became blindingly illuminated….an army of cluster-wink sea-snails, their bio-luminescent shells acting as magnifying mirrors of pure green light, poured in through the sub-caves, the Bishop-Fish, swam among them, helping her gather the scrolls and assisted her back to the surface.

Reaching air and dry ground, she collapsed in a faint, unable to detect the force of the rumbling sea bearing down on the horizon or the screams of the Acolytes and Anchorites from the Coracle portholes trying to alert her. The row of un-sailing souls facing the skyline at high ground sang a hymn of such penetrating beauty, but Roe's ears were closed, her eyes unfocused, she lost consciousness.

A sharp bite grabbed her by the neck, lifting her, half dragging and heaving her up cliffs, roughly hauling her over rocks and dumping her down. The Wolf. Many hands then grabbed her suddenly, pulling her forward, and up, she began to rouse, lurched onto the Coracle below-deck, as the men began to chop at the mirror threads, the ropes chimed as if broken glass and the hymn and the roar of the sea rose and rose and finally entered her senses.

Roe's last sight of Old Earth was of the Wolf bounding away to the hills. In a pithy backwards glance, they exchanged a thousand words. He sprang away, but she knew he would be watching from above as he faced his demise against the forces of nature.

Tumbling further into the chaos aboard the Coracle, a new face hovered over her, reaching out a hand. Roe sat up, dazed, a pelt of books over one shoulder, on the other shoulder a fishing net full of scrolls, the central wooden umbilicus sticks unravelling to reveal holes along their slender spines as if musical instruments.

"…*she will raise a vault of flutes…and nets of …knowledge*…You must be Roe."

Over the deafening roar of the tsunami about to hit outside, the fifty sailors held tight inside, hands looped in ropes, awaiting the lift upon the new sea….ready for take-off…birds squawked across the Arks roof, axes chopped glass threads, animals brayed, and men and women cried, prayed, sang and cheered.

Roe took her hand. "And you, must be Orla".

EPILOGUE

The Bishop-Fish took off her hood and looked out at the stars from her invisible rocky perch. She saw the Wolf and the Selkie, the Selkie mother and the Fisherman, the Selkie grandfather and the young Anchorites and their stories, the Ferryman and the Bailiff and the Masons and Boat Builders, their families, Orla and the Brotherhood of Men, the Priestesses' and their symbols.

She saw past the Earth, to the moon and out to the planets and saw the atoms of stardust dispersing and re-forming, she blinked and another Millenium or two passed again. The all-seeing eyes closed for night's rest and the Bishop-Fish reached for a fresh piece of paper.

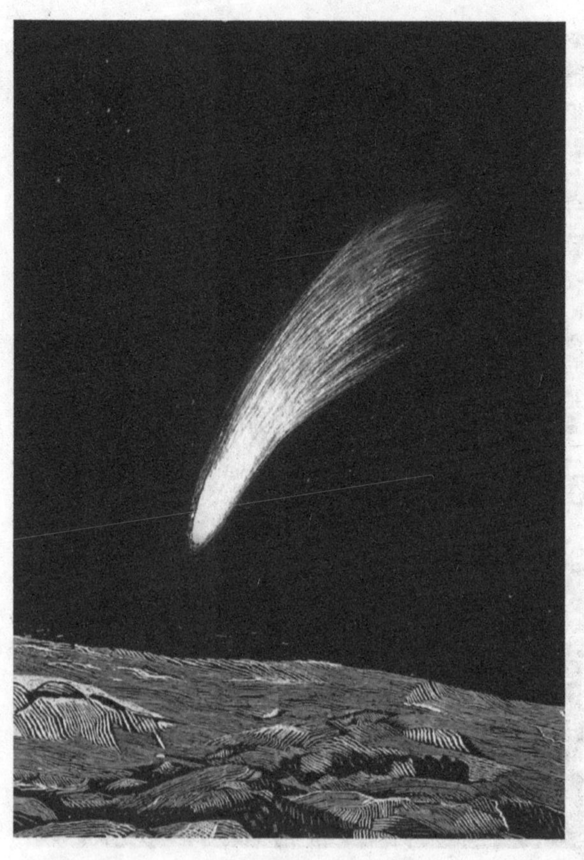

The End.

ABOUT THE AUTHOR

Kelsey Ashe grew up between the remote wild
West coast of Tasmania and the Southern Alps of
New Zealand and now lives in the port of Fremantle,
Western Australia with her husband and two children.
Ashe creates worlds; *Imaginary Aesthetic Territories* of
vivid Antipodean terrains in large format hand-etched
screen-prints, short films and surrealist fiction.

Her artwork and prose is characterised by
"piercing graphic narratives" and "fervently wavering
archetypal symbols" that seek *yūgen*; a term within
Japanese aesthetic philosophy which refers to the
dark, tranquil colour of the universe. Calm and deep,
yūgen is the profound awareness of creation that
triggers a deep emotional and spiritual response.

Ashe's surrealist film, the audio-visual poem and
screenplay *Pearls and Blackbirds* placed her in the 2020
international all-female surrealist exhibition *31 Women*;
curated by Dr. Catriona McAra (UK).

Ashe exhibits her screen prints and films regularly,
nationally and internationally and frequently publishes
essays and poems. She has also edited a poetry
anthology titled *Dark Seas; Collected Poems of the
Wonderous Deep*, published a monograph; *Archetype*
and has a PhD (Art).

The Deep Green Sea is Ashe's first novella.

FROM THE AUTHOR

In July 2023, I wrote the first draft of The Deep Green Sea - imagining a world where a child of formidable resilience is born of the sea. I emailed a friend the draft about a Selkie "…*with the highly unusual condition where its seal fur was inside out and separate to the body, like an external organ that hung attached at the back of the neck like a loose cape…*"
Just one month later, my own daughter was diagnosed with a malignant brainstem tumour.
She survived but lost her ability to walk.
It appeared suddenly as if the 'tale' I had written was a kind of mythopoetic premonition where not only had I imagined the exact place of her wound as a sacred marking, but had prepared the map and raft for navigating the unbearable.
I finished the book beside her hospital bed, day after day, night after night, through a full year of excruciating treatment. What began as a fairytale became, unknowingly the memento of an immense soul voyage woven in real time.
This book is not only fiction. It is a soul artifact, a record of hope, grief, transformation — and the loving act of wrapping something in myth and sacredness rather than chaos and despair.
May it carry you too, if you ever find yourself adrift, tangled in the weeds and far from shore.

I would love to hear from you.

Thank you so much for reading my book, it really
does mean the world to me; I love to see who it's
reaching across this wide world.
If you enjoyed it or found it inspiring would you
take a moment to tell me!? Your feedback helps
others find this story and allows me to understand
what my audience appreciates.

Simply scan this code below to tap directly
through to my Amazon Review page.

Your kind words go a long way, thanks
for your support.
Love Kelsey Ashe XX

Discover more about
Kelsey Ashe

www.kelseyashe.com

@worldofashe